The Turtle Pirates

Beneath the Sunrise

Ben Swiercz

For Grandma Edie

Acknowledgements

I owe many thanks to Talitha Shipman for her wonderful cover art and design, as well as to Patricia Cone for her insightful editing. Mostly, I want to thank Emerson and Whitney for inspiring my ideas, supporting my writing, and always motivating me to be the best version of myself.

A Note on Door County, Wisconsin

While Door County is a very real place, most of the locations in *The Turtle Pirates* are fictional. This book is not meant to portray an exact replica of the real Door County, but instead show a version that stays true to its character while better fitting a middle grade story. Friendly people, boating, beaches, fishing, excellent food, beautiful nature, a lively arts scene, and of course—lighthouses, are all part of what makes Door County a special place to live or visit.

A Note on Speech Disorders

A common struggle for people with speech disorders is that while they know in their thoughts how a word should sound, they have trouble saying it correctly. Evey, the main character in *The Turtle Pirates*, has such a disorder. Speaking clearly often requires her to focus and talk slowly. Here are a few notes about how I reflect this in the book:

An em dash (—) shows an interruption or quick change of direction in a sentence. I mostly use this when Evey realizes she said a word wrong and tries to correct herself.

An ellipsis (. . .) shows a pause. I mostly use this when Evey pauses to focus on saying a difficult word correctly.

Words are sometimes misspelled to show when Evey mispronounces a word, usually by leaving out a hard-to-say sound, or swapping it with an easier one.

CHAPTER 1

Evey raised her right eyebrow. *Why is the room red?* she thought. She looked around and saw a glowing light coming from the closet, but it quickly disappeared. *Must have been Alex's phone,* she thought as she listened to her cousin snoring in the bunk above her.

Evey turned her attention to the lumpy bed as she squirmed under the sheets. After a minute of trying to find a comfortable spot, she sighed and opened her eyes. Her thoughts returned to her latest speech blunder at dinner a few hours earlier.

Can I have a mushroom booger? Evey thought, replaying her order to the waiter. *Burger—the word is burger—why is that so hard to pronounce! The waiter nearly fell over. The whole family laughed at me. I am so tired of this! How slow do I have to talk to not make these stupid mistakes!* Evey ground her teeth. *And it doesn't help that Mom and Dad always have to comment,* she thought. *Saying 'it's fine' and 'just talk slower' doesn't help when I can tell they're embarrassed by me!*

A gust of wind rattled the bedroom window. Evey wiped a few tears from her eyes and turned to look. Outside, the tree branches rocked back-and-forth. Large waves rolled across the lake. Dark gray clouds raced through the sky. *Why does this have to happen now?* Evey thought. *Vacation at Grandpa's is supposed to be a time I can forget that I talk like a toddler.* Evey wiped away more tears. *Whatever,* she thought, *I don't need to talk to my family. That's what facial expressions are for.*

Evey watched a gap in the clouds reveal the bright, full moon. The red glow returned. *That can't be Alex's phone,* she thought. Curious, she rolled out of bed. *Ouch!* she thought as she stubbed a toe on Alex's suitcase. She quietly pushed it aside and tiptoed to the closet.

The red glow came from a partially opened drawer in an old dresser. Evey sat down and grabbed the drawer's handle. As she gently pulled it open, the light grew so bright she had to turn away. Once her eyes adjusted, she peered in.

Is that what I think it is? Evey thought. She reached into the drawer and pulled out a red crystal necklace. *Grandma's crystal—nobody told me this thing glows. I probably wouldn't have stuffed it in a drawer and forgot about it if somebody did.* Evey held her hand in front of her face to shield her eyes from the bright light. *Seriously, does this thing have a battery in it?* she thought. She closed her hand around the crystal to block the glowing light. She moved it back-and-forth inside her fist to inspect it. It felt jagged, about the size of a golf ball, and it was attached to a string necklace. When not glowing, Evey remembered it having a dull, light red color.

Evey closed the drawer and carried the crystal back to her bed. *That's weird,* she thought as the red glow disappeared. After a few seconds, it returned. Evey looked at the window and noticed another cloud racing past the moon. She moved the crystal in-and-out of the light, making the glow come and go.

So, the moonlight makes it glow—like it's a werewolf—this is weird, Evey thought. She searched her brain for an explanation, but could only remember what her dad said when he gave her the crystal the year before. *Red, rough, and beautiful,* she thought, reciting the way he described it. He said it reminded him of both Evey and her grandma. While she died before Evey was born, her dad told her that they shared the same short red hair, blue eyes, and feisty attitude.

Evey brought the crystal closer to her face. Sparkles of red light seemingly danced inside of it. Her surroundings faded from her sight. The noise of the wind outside disappeared. Her breathing slowed, her mind went blank, and her eyelids grew heavy.

A rush of air across Evey's back stirred her out of the trance. She sat upright and opened her eyes. Her vision was blurry, but she recognized the red glow of the crystal by her feet. She grabbed it, but scooped up a handful of sand too.

CHAPTER 2

A cold wave of water sprayed Evey's back. "Ahh!" she yelled as she scrambled up the sand. She reached a grassy spot, then turned around. Instead of lying on her lumpy bed, she found herself sitting on a beach. The choppy water sent waves crashing at her feet. Above, dark clouds flew through the night sky. *Where am I?* Evey thought. *Is this the lake? Where are the houses? Why are there no lights anywhere?*

Evey looked at her grandma's crystal. Resting in the palm of her hand, the glow had disappeared. Evey turned to the sky and saw the moon was hidden behind the clouds. *What is this thing?* she thought as she put the crystal necklace on. *Couldn't Grandma have just left me a cool globe instead?*

Evey closed her eyes and listened carefully for the sounds of cars, boats, or people, but she only heard the wind and crashing waves. She turned away from the water and saw a wall of tall grass covered in fog. *I'm just dreaming, right?* she thought. She rubbed her eyes to try to wake up, but stopped when a loud howl rang through the air. *What was that?* Another howl followed. Then a third. Then so many that Evey could not count them. She held her breath until the howls stopped. *Stay calm,* she thought. *It's just a dream. A weird and very realistic dream, but totally safe and—*

Another series of howls shot through the air. *Dream?* Evey thought. *More like a nightmare!* She walked backward until her feet touched the cold water. *No way I'm swimming in that*, she thought as she watched the waves.

Another howl, louder than before, made Evey look back at the tall grass. She bit her lip. Her hands began to shake, and her heart pounded in her chest. Her eyes darted back-and-forth until she found a lone tree in the distance, barely visible through the fog. *Run! Go for it!* she thought as she tried to force her legs to move.

A series of growls screamed out of the grass. Evey's legs snapped into action, and she took off toward the tree. The tall grass slapped her face as she sprinted through the fog. When the grass gave way and the tree appeared, she jumped, grabbed a branch, pulled herself up, and started climbing. After a minute, she stopped to catch her breath, then looked down. A blanket of fog and leaves covered the tall grass. Evey crouched for a better look, but a gust of wind violently shook the tree and nearly sent her tumbling out. She reached for a nearby branch to steady herself. She clutched the bark so hard it scratched her hands. The cold wind made her wet skin feel like ice, sending shivers through her body. She breathed so rapidly that she felt lightheaded. *I'm only twelve*, she thought. *I'm too young for this crap!*

Evey closed her eyes and focused on slowing her breathing. When the wind finally stopped, she opened her eyes. *I'm on an island*, she thought as she studied the view from the tree. *How is that possible? Did I sleep-swim here? Is that a thing people do?* Evey thought that the oval-shaped island looked about twice the size of the running track at her school. The fog made it difficult to see anything other than the narrow beach along the island's edge. Evey tried to scan the island's foggy center, but a strong beam of light made her turn away. She shielded her eyes until it passed, then watched it move in a slow circle. *Where is that coming—*

A bell in the distance cut off Evey's train of thought. *Ding, ding!* it repeated. She looked toward the beach. The bright light moved over the area, briefly revealing a dock.

A dock and a bell, Evey thought. *That means a boat— hopefully one not filled with werewolves, coyotes, or whatever else was trying to eat me.* Evey climbed down the tree, but stopped on the lowest branch and bit her lip. After hearing nothing, she carefully slid off the branch and dropped to the ground with a loud thud. She ran through the long grass toward the dock.

The bell rang again just as Evey reached the beach. *That has to be a boat out there,* she thought as she stared at the fog-covered water. *I guess there's only one way to find out.* She slowly took a step out of the grass and onto the sand.

"This isn't right," said a deep voice.

Evey stumbled and fell to the sand. She turned in the direction of the voice and saw a dark figure emerge from the tall grass. It looked like the shadow of a man. Evey could only make out the shape of bulky boots, a long coat, and a tricorn hat.

"This night feels familiar—like a memory," said the shadowy man as he looked around the beach. He turned to Evey. "But I am quite certain you were not here."

Evey sat frozen on the ground until her grandma's crystal began to glow, forcing her to shield her eyes.

"The crystal—how did you . . ." began the shadowy man.

6

How did I what? Evey thought. She shook her head. *Who cares what he said! Run back into the grass!* She tried to stand, but her legs felt numb. *So, running is apparently out,* she thought. *Okay, then just say something!* Evey tried to speak, but her jaw felt locked shut. *Why does this always happen? Talk, Evey!*

The shadowy man kneeled on the ground. "Sorry for frightening you," he said. "The crystal startled me. There is something quite peculiar about it. I find it hard to explain, but every time I've seen it, it feels as if I'm reliving a . . . memory. It's almost as if that crystal carries a piece of me."

Evey raised her eyebrow. *Who is this person, and what in the world is he talking about?* she thought.

"I do suspect," continued the shadowy man, "that the crystal must have something to do with the secret."

Evey raised her eyebrow higher. *Secret?* she thought. *Should I be excited instead of scared?*

The shadowy man tilted his head to the left. "Is something the matter with your eyebrow, young lady?"

Evey rolled her eyes. *If something is wrong here,* she thought, *it's definitely with you—Mr. Shadow—and your creepy island!*

The shadowy man repeated his question.

Evey sighed and rubbed her jaw. "It's easy—I mean . . . easier than . . . words. I meant to ask . . . what the . . . secret. What is it?"

"Something of great importance—great beauty—great power."

Does this guy only speak in riddles? Evey thought. *I thought I was hard to understand.*

"The secret is complex," continued the shadowy man. "To tell you would only confuse you. I'm afraid the only way to truly understand is to experience it yourself."

Sorry Mr. Shadow, but I'm already confused, Evey thought.

"The crystal is both a map and key," said the shadowy man. "Listen to it and it will guide you to the secret. When you find it, the crystal will unlock it."

That doesn't help either, Evey thought, *but at least I'm better at listening than talking.* She rubbed her jaw. "You mean a . . . treasure?" she asked.

"You could say that, but it's worth far more than money."

And back to the riddles, Evey thought. *Riddle me this, Mr. Shadow—how do I get off this island?* She took a deep breath. "Why . . . me? Why am I dear—I mean . . . here?"

"That question, I fear, I cannot answer. You are not the first person I have seen with that crystal. In fact, I must say you bear a striking resemblance to one of the others. But whatever the reason, be it chance or destiny, that crystal is yours now. You must decide what to do with it."

"Huh," Evey mumbled as she looked at the glowing crystal dangling from her neck. *I have to be hallucinating*, she thought. She looked back at the shadowy man and slowly opened her mouth. "How do I . . . find it?"

The shadowy man pointed to the light circling the island. "There," he said.

Evey turned to the light and shielded her face as it passed over her. "What is it?" she asked, turning back to the shadowy man.

"The sunrise—look beneath it," he said.

Evey raised her eyebrow again. *Sunrise? Listen to the crystal?* she thought. *I may not be able to talk right, but I still make more sense than—*

Boom! A distant, loud rumble shot through the air. A series of small popping noises followed. The shadowy man stood up. "I'm afraid I must move quickly," he said. "I must try to stop them." He turned and walked toward the dock.

"Wait," Evey mumbled. She rubbed her jaw. "Can't you day—I mean . . . say . . . more?"

The shadowy man stopped and turned. "I wish I could, young lady. But as I said, this is all a memory—an old one. Memories grow foggy over time. Much like the fog covering this island." The man took another look around the beach, then turned back to Evey. "Remember—look *beneath the sunrise.*"

What is he talking about? Evey thought. She tried to speak, but her jaw stiffened. She watched the shadowy man walk onto the dock and disappear in the fog. She tried to run after him, but her legs felt stuck. The bright light passed over her and turned everything white. She covered her face and fell to her knees.

CHAPTER 3

Evey opened her eyes to see the sun shining through the bedroom window. She pulled the blanket over her face. After a few seconds, she sat up and banged her head on the top bunk with a loud thud.

Dang it, she thought as she rubbed her throbbing scalp.

Evey felt her heart racing rapidly as she checked her surroundings. She was back in the bedroom, with Alex snoring above her. Outside the window, streaks of purple and pink covered the early morning sky. It was her family's last day at her grandpa's lake house in Door County, Wisconsin. Her parents took her there to spend the first week of every summer. Her cousin, aunt, and uncle always joined them.

What a weird dream, Evey thought. *It felt so real. More like a—what did that shadowy guy call it—a memory. And what was up with that light at the end?* Evey touched her face. It felt unusually warm, as if the bright light had given her a sunburn. *I think that dream means it's time for me to go home.*

Evey rubbed her eyes, then looked around the room. A lighthouse painting on the wall caught her attention. She had seen it hundreds of times, but never paid much attention to it. This time, she noticed the bright light shining across the water. *Grandma really had a thing for lighthouses,* Evey thought. *Wait, the light on the island—was it a lighthouse?* Evey pulled herself out of bed and walked over to the picture. *That has to be it,* she thought as she felt the painting's rough texture. *Was I staring at this before I fell asleep? Maybe that caused the dream.*

Alex rustled the sheets in the top bunk, then started snoring louder. Evey rolled her eyes. *Or a week sleeping below Alex is just driving me crazy,* she thought.

Evey took a deep breath, then remembered her grandma's crystal. *But that doesn't explain the crystal glowing,* she thought. *And what did that shadowy guy say about it?* She took the jagged crystal off from around her neck. Without the glow, it was the dull, light red color she remembered. *Maybe the glowing was part of my dream*, she thought. *No, it can't be. I know I was awake when it lit up the room.* Evey bit her lip. *What's happening to me?*

Evey left the bedroom and walked to the screened porch overlooking the yard, dock, and Turtle Lake. She took a seat in a wicker chair and watched the rising sun's golden reflection on the water.

The sound of snoring made Evey turn toward the bedrooms. She laughed quietly as she tried to guess how much longer Alex and her grandpa would sleep. *What's the point of a lake house if you never watch the sunrise?* she thought. *Wait—sunrise—that's it!* The details rushed back to Evey. She remembered the long grass, the howling, and the shadowy man mentioning a secret. *If that light on the island was a lighthouse,* she thought, *then that's what he meant when he said 'sunrise.' And it will lead me to the secret if I*

11

look beneath it—whatever that means. I should write this down.

Evey ran to the kitchen to grab a pen and paper. She returned to the porch and wrote until her hand cramped. As she finished, she heard a familiar tapping on the wood floor. Her grandpa's Goldendoodle, Howie, trotted toward her. He greeted Evey with a wag of his tail and a snuggle against her legs.

"Hey, Howie," she said as she pet his shaggy, white fur. Howie walked to the front door, then returned with his leash in his mouth. "Sure," Evey said as she wrapped the leash around his neck. She opened the porch door. Howie darted outside and buried his nose in the grass, sniffing everything in sight.

After a few minutes in the front yard, Evey gently tugged Howie's leash. "The lake," she said. The two strolled down the long yard toward the water. Evey took a seat on the bench at the end of the dock while Howie finished sniffing the yard.

Evey scanned Turtle Lake. She started at the south end, where the water extended to a wall of evergreen trees about two miles away. Next, she looked east to the opposite shoreline, but the rising sun made her shield her eyes. Finally, she turned to the north where she saw the highway bridge about a mile away. A small truck slowly crossed the bridge. *Must be a fisherman to be out this early on a Saturday,* she thought.

Quack! Quack! A group of ducks flew across the water. Evey spotted them as they splashed down near the lake's island. She watched them until they disappeared under some fallen tree trunks.

I don't think that island could be any different from the one last night, Evey thought. As far as she knew, Turtle Lake's island had no official name. It was long and covered with tall trees. A small, rocky beach at the northern end was the only good spot to land a boat on it.

Evey heard Howie's paws tapping on the dock as he trotted to the bench. He sat down next to her feet and searched the lake for the ducks. "I can't remember . . . seeing the lake so calm," Evey said. "It's so . . . shallow, but it . . . amazes me how big the . . . waves can get."

Howie looked at Evey briefly, then turned back to the water.

"Don't mind me," Evey said. "You're . . . easier to talk to . . . than people. You don't care if I . . . pause or ness—I mean . . . mess up my . . . words."

While bending over to pet Howie, something caught Evey's eye. She looked up and noticed a lone kayaker near the northern end of the island. "That looks like Grandpa's red . . . kayak," she said.

The kayaker waved in Evey's direction.

"Must be Mom or Dad," she said as she waved back. "But aren't . . . they biking . . . this morning?"

Evey noticed Howie staring at the yard. She turned in the same direction. Next to the shed stood all four of her grandpa's kayaks—yellow, blue, green, and the red one.

"Okay, so I'm . . . waving at a . . . stranger." Evey turned back to the lake, but the kayaker had disappeared. "Where'd . . . they go?"

Howie cocked his head.

Evey scanned the lake for a minute, then reclined on the bench and sighed. *I think I need my head examined,* she thought. She looked at her grandpa's kayaks and bit her lip.

Howie growled.

"What?" Evey said. "I'll wear a life . . . vest. And Grandpa's till in bed—I mean . . . still."

Howie snorted as Evey jogged to the shed. She opened the door, grabbed a life vest and paddle, then dragged the heavy, twelve-foot, red kayak toward the lake. She set it on the edge of the dock, then carefully lowered it in.

"Wait here," Evey said as she tied Howie's leash to the dock. Howie whined. Evey remembered her dad telling her that her grandma used to kayak with Howie. "Maybe next time," she said. She patted Howie's head, then hopped into the kayak.

Evey pushed away from the dock and started paddling toward the north end of the island. She tried to move fast to catch up to the mystery kayaker. However, it had been a year since she last kayaked, so the boat moved unevenly as she struggled to find a rhythm.

After a few minutes, Evey stopped for a break. While the air was cool, the sun's reflection on the lake made it feel much warmer. Sweat already covered her forehead and hands. She took a few deep breaths while watching the scenery.

Why can't we get a sailboat up here, Evey thought as she rubbed her sore arms. *That would be so much easier!* She shook each of her arms out, then started paddling slowly. She made sure to dip the entire paddle into the water using a smooth stroke to minimize drag. After a minute, she found a good rhythm and sped up.

Once near the wooded island, Evey noticed that a gray rock wall covered in roots and weeds provided the only break from the trees. She guessed it stood nearly ten feet above the water. She paddled closer to the island to look for turtles hiding among the fallen tree trunks. Despite Turtle Lake's name, Evey had never actually seen one there.

After finding nothing, Evey continued paddling north. *That kayaker has to be up here somewhere*, she thought. *At least if I see somebody, I'll know I don't need my head checked.* She passed the last few trees blocking her view of the north side of the lake. She turned the kayak to the right. *And . . . nothing*, she thought as she looked at the empty water.

Evey kept paddling until she approached the northeast corner of the island. The island was much longer from north to south than east to west, so she reached the corner quickly. She rounded it and saw the entire eastern side of the lake, but only found a fishing boat. *Unless the kayak transformed into that fishing boat*, she thought, *I officially do need my head checked.*

Having given up on the mystery kayaker, Evey turned around. She paddled back to the northwest corner of the island, then stopped for another break. Looking toward her grandpa's dock, she spotted Howie, who looked like a small, white dot.

This must be where the kayaker was, Evey thought as she waved in Howie's direction. *Maybe I'm just seeing things because I'm worked up over that dream. Yea, it's probably just that—I hope.*

Evey turned back to the island. The small beach caught her eye. It spanned about thirty feet across, and consisted of a mixture of pebbles and sand. Thick trees and large rocks sat on each end of it. Something about area gave Evey an odd feeling. Staring at it, she felt her mind lose focus. She sensed a thought that she could not put to words. As she tried to focus on it, the thought turned into a voice that kept repeating louder and louder in her head.

You've been here before! Evey finally heard. A flash of images flooded her mind. She saw herself sitting in the kayak in the same spot, but with Howie. She saw a shiny reflection in the water, then herself plunging in with a mask and snorkel. She swam to the bottom of the lake. She saw her arm reach under a rock and pull out a hard object. She brushed the sand and mud away from it to reveal her grandma's red crystal.

CHAPTER 4

Evey jerked her kayak so hard it almost flipped over. After steadying it, she looked around. She was alone on the lake, near the island. In the distance, she saw Howie sitting on her grandpa's dock.

I've been here before? Evey thought. Her feeling of déjà vu was strong. *I guess I have been here before, but I know I've never gone swimming here.* She replayed the vision of jumping in the water and grabbing the crystal, then remembered her dad telling her that her grandma found the crystal in the lake. *That's it*, Evey thought. *I'm probably remembering that story. I wonder if this is where Grandma found the crystal.*

Evey paddled to the island. She jumped out of the kayak and dragged it onto the rocky beach. She opened the kayak's storage compartment and pulled out a mask and snorkel.

Good thing the parents aren't here, Evey thought as she took her life vest off. She put the mask and snorkel on, waded into the water, took a deep breath, and dove in. She swam a few feet, then popped her head up and let out a shivering cry as the cold water engulfed her body.

The lake always feels like ice in the morning, Evey thought, remembering her grandpa's warning. She adjusted her mask and snorkel, then dove down. Ignoring the stinging pain from the cold water, she searched the area for anything shiny. She looked on all sides of a big, algae covered rock, but found nothing. She returned to the surface for air, then dove back down and moved the smaller rocks around. After several more dives, she checked the last of the rocks. Coming up empty, she swam back to the island.

An uneasy feeling overtook Evey as she put her snorkeling gear away. *Something about this place does seem familiar,* she thought as she stared at the island's thick, tangled trees. *I feel like I have been here before, which is weird since I know I've never actually set foot on this jungle-looking island.* Evey watched the tree leaves move gently in the wind, but saw nothing else. She heard birds chirping and crickets buzzing, but nothing unusual.

Whack! Whack! Bright neon paint hit Evey's kayak and splattered all over her red hair. She turned around and saw a small sailboat approaching the island. Its mast held two large, white sails. Four boys around her age stood along the side of the boat. After dropping an anchor and lowering the sails, the boys jumped off and walked to the beach.

Evey tried to open her mouth, but her jaw stiffened.

"You want to tell us what you're doing here?" asked one of the boys. He looked to be the leader of the group. His messy, brown hair covered part of his face, but Evey could still see his green eyes staring at her. "We're waiting!" the boy yelled.

Evey clenched her fists. She tried to think of a quick response, but could not put any words together.

"What's the matter—are you too stupid to talk?" the leader said, causing his friends to laugh.

Evey's fists ached as she tightened them. *I'm not stupid, you jerk!* she thought, but she struggled to open her mouth. *Say something to him! Talk!* She rubbed her jaw until she could finally move it. "I was wimming," she mumbled.

"Wimming?" the leader said through a laugh.

Evey ground her teeth. Her jaw hurt. *Say it right, Evey!* she thought. "Swim . . . ing," she said.

"This is our island," the leader replied, "and we don't like tourists like you *wimming* around it." The boys laughed again.

If I can't talk, fine—I'll just punch him, Evey thought. She raised her right fist and stomped toward the leader, but another boy shot her stomach with his paintball gun. The sharp pain knocked her backward. She fell to her knees with neon paint covering her shirt.

The group laughed again.

Evey wiped the paint from her shirt. *Wasn't paintball a thing back when my parents were kids,* she thought. She stood up and scowled at the group.

"What are you going to do—fight us all?" the leader said.

Evey looked at the four boys, then put her head down. *No, I'm definitely not*, she thought. She unclenched her firsts and walked to her kayak. "I'll . . . leave," she mumbled, fighting back tears.

"Whoa, wait a minute," the leader said. He and the other boys moved between Evey and the water. "You don't get off that easy. Trespassers go to the cliff."

Evey raised her eyebrow.

Two of the boys took her kayak and started walking along a path into the trees. The boy with the paintball gun pointed it at Evey. "Start walking," he said.

Evey followed the boys down the narrow path. *No point trying to run away without my kayak,* she thought as she scanned the woods surrounding her. She rubbed her temples. *Why didn't I say something!* she thought. *I shouldn't let these punks talk to me like that.* She ground her teeth. *Although, maybe they're right to call me stupid. I can't put a sentence together to save my—*

Crack! Evey tripped on a tree root and fell face first in the dirt. The boys laughed loudly. "Come on, we don't have all day!" one yelled.

Evey picked herself up and brushed the dirt off. The boy with the paintball gun motioned for her to keep walking. She put her head down to avoid tripping the rest of the way. After several minutes, the path ended at a clearing high above the water. Evey recognized "the cliff" as the rock wall she saw while kayaking.

Looks a lot higher from up here, Evey thought as she peered over the edge.

Two of the boys brushed past her and hurled her kayak into the lake. "Hey!" she yelled as it splashed into the water.

The leader stepped forward. "Like I told you, we can't just let you paddle out of here without punishment. Trespassers have to jump."

Evey shook her head no.

The leader smirked. "Either you jump or we shoot paintballs at you until you fall in. Personally, I'd be happy to see you covered in paint."

Evey glared at the leader. She cleared her mind to think of something to say. Finally, settling on the right words, she opened her mouth.

Splat! Splat! The boy with the paintball gun shot at Evey's feet before she could speak. Her hands shaking, she turned to the water. *What is going on?* she thought. *I've never even seen a rude person in Door County, but now I'm being thrown off an island!*

"Let's go!" yelled one boy. "Hurry up!" shouted another.

Evey closed her eyes, took a deep breath, bent her legs, and jumped. The cold water shocked her skin as she crashed into the lake. She sunk a few feet, then shot to the surface and gasped for air. Shivering, she wiped the water from her eyes.

The leader leaned over the edge of the cliff. "Is it chilly?" he said. He laughed with his friends, then turned back to Evey. "Have fun *wimming* home!"

Evey watched the boys walk away. She could still hear them after they disappeared behind the trees. "Did you see her face?" said one boy. "What a loser!" said another.

Once the voices faded, Evey swam to her life vest and put it on. She grabbed the paddle and brought it over to the kayak. She tried to pull herself into the seat, but the kayak flipped over on top of her. After several more failed attempts to climb in, she punched the side of the kayak until her hand hurt.

I screwed up! Evey thought as she tried to stop herself from crying. *I can't go back without the kayak! My parents will never let me hear the end of it. Why didn't I fight those kids! Why didn't I yell at them! And why can't I say "swimming" like a normal person!*

Exhausted and angry, Evey floated on her back and stared at the blue sky. Tears filled her eyes, then rolled down her cheeks.

CHAPTER 5

Evey floated in the lake for several minutes before she heard a voice in the distance. She turned her body upright to look around. She saw a boy around her age approaching in a purple kayak.

"Need some help?" the boy asked.

Evey shook her head yes.

The boy maneuvered his kayak next to Evey's and helped her flip it over. He set his paddle across both boats, then held on to the side of Evey's. "It's a lot easier to get back in with two people," he said.

Evey used the boy's paddle to pull herself out of the water, then wiggled onto the kayak while he held it steady. She turned her legs around and dropped them into the opening. "Tanks," she said.

"No problem," the boy replied. "I saw you struggling to get back in. To do it yourself, you have to climb on the back of the boat, not the side. My parents don't like me kayaking alone, but I do it anyway. So, they taught me how to get back in by myself in case I flip over. I'm really good at it now— which is what I tell them every time they get mad at me for kayaking by myself. It's a vicious cycle. I don't know why they . . ."

Evey blankly stared at the boy as he rambled. *What is he talking about?* she thought.

"Anyway," the boy said, "you must be freezing. You probably don't need to hear me talk on and on. It's what I do when I meet new people. I don't know why I do it. I guess I'm nervous or—jeez, I'm doing it again—sorry. You okay by the way? You're shivering."

Evey nodded. *He looks familiar,* she thought as she noticed his brown eyes, patch of freckles on his nose and cheeks, and black hair sticking out from the edges of a Chicago Bears hat. *Oh no! He's the kid with the bow!* Evey felt her face turn red as she remembered kayaking with her parents the previous summer. She had noticed the boy shooting a bow and arrow in his yard near the shore. She was staring at him when he suddenly turned to look at her. She jerked so hard that she flipped her kayak over and fell into the water. *It's okay,* Evey thought. *He probably doesn't recognize me.*

"You know, you and your kayak look familiar," the boy said. "Didn't I see you take a spill in the lake last year?"

Evey looked down and squeezed her oar. *And he does remember,* she thought. *That figures given how this morning has gone.*

"Hopefully," the boy continued, "the next time I see you won't involve you falling into the water."

Evey faked a smile.

The boy scratched his neck. "Was that mean?" he asked. "It sounds like it could be mean. I'm sorry either way. I say things without thinking, in addition to rambling."

I don't know what's worse, Evey thought, *not being able to talk, or not being able to stop talking.*

"You can talk, right?" The boy covered his mouth as soon as he finished the sentence. "Sorry!" he mumbled through his hands. "That definitely sounded mean."

"It's . . . fine," Evey said as she rubbed her jaw. "I . . . talk. It's just . . . hard."

"Like a speech disorder?" the boy asked.

"I'm not dupid!" Evey snapped.

The boy flinched. "I should probably stop talking now."

Evey shook her head. "It's not you," she said. "Those kids called me . . . stupid. I'm just . . . mad. I do have a . . . disorder. I have to pause or I . . . say . . . things . . . wrong. Especially . . . when . . . mad."

"Oh, good. Not you being mad—that stinks. I'd be mad too. I saw what those punks did to you. But good that you talk. And I can understand you fine. Besides, I can talk enough for both of us. I'm Archer, by the way. I always forget to tell people my name. My mom says it's the first thing you should do when you meet somebody. Oh, and shake their hand." Archer extended his hand toward Evey.

"Evey," she said as she shook his hand. "What's your . . . first name?"

"Archer is my first name," he said with an eye roll.

"Oh, sorry. You must get . . . that a lot."

"It's okay. I'm Archer the archer." Archer positioned his arms as if shooting an arrow into the lake.

Evey smiled.

"You should meet my little brother," Archer said. "His name is Baker and he loves to bake."

Evey raised her eyebrow.

"I'm just kidding. His name is Rowan and he loves to row boats."

Evey raised her eyebrow as far as it would go.

Archer laughed and confessed, "I don't even have a brother! I have two older sisters. They're twins, but like way older. They're in college, so I don't see them that much. And I actually like badminton better than archery. I'm a beast with a racquet. Next year, I'm going to win the tournament at my school. I just have to get by—jeez, I'm rambling again—sorry."

Evey shrugged. She looked toward her grandpa's house. Howie still sat by the edge of the dock. "I . . . should go," she said.

"Where do you live?" Archer asked.

Evey pointed at the dock. "My grandpa's house is dare—I mean . . . there. With . . . the dog."

"Cool, I'm just a few houses away."

The two paddled toward the shore. By now, the sun loomed high in the sky and the air felt much warmer. Evey finally stopped shivering once her clothes dried. Her jaw relaxed, but felt sore. "Do you know those ids . . . kids, I mean?" she asked Archer.

"Yea, they're the East Siders—well, that's what I call them—they all live on the East side of the lake. I've seen as many as six of them on the boat at one time. I don't know their real names, except for Finn. He's their leader."

"Does he have the . . . messy, brown . . . hair?"

"That and a real attitude."

"When do . . . they leave?"

Archer groaned. "They're always here. They live here year-round."

Evey remembered Finn complaining about tourists. "Do you live ear—I mean . . . here . . . all year?" she asked.

Archer pointed to his Bears hat. "Do I look like a Green Bay Packers fan?"

"Oh," Evey said.

"My dad says I'm brave," Archer said as he adjusted his hat. "He always tells me about this time he went to a Bears-Packers game in Green Bay when he was little. He was all decked out in Bears gear, and some giant man in a hunting outfit spilled his food on him after the Bears scored a touchdown. The man said it was an accident, but my dad thinks he did it on purpose. He still gets mad about it."

Evey chuckled. "Why do . . . those . . . kids act like . . . that?" she asked.

"I don't know," Archer replied. "I tried to talk to them last year, but they shot a bunch of paintballs at me. I just assumed they're big Packers fans and saw my Bears hat. I don't suppose you trash-talked the Packers, did you?"

Evey shook her head no. *If only I could trash-talk*, she thought. "They called me a . . . tourist."

"Interesting," Archer said. "Their issue isn't with Bears fans, but tourists. They must have some tragic backstory to explain that."

Evey raised her eyebrow.

"Like in movies," Archer continued. "Maybe Finn's dog was hit by a driver from Illinois, so he swore revenge on us all!"

Evey raised her other eyebrow.

"Is something wrong with your eyebrows?" Archer asked. "Jeez, that was mean again. Sorry, it's just that it kind of looks like they're twitching."

"Huh?" Evey replied as she lowered her eyebrows. She felt her face turn red. "It's just . . . easier . . . than talking."

"Oh, I get it. It's like body language for asking a question. I was afraid you were having an allergic reaction. It's pretty clever, actually. Sometimes, I feel like I waste a lot of breath talking so much. Maybe I should use my eyebrow." Archer looked up as he struggled to raise either of his eyebrows, causing Evey to laugh. "Maybe not," Archer said. "Anyway, what was I saying?"

"East . . . Siders," Evey said.

"Right! My mom always says people have logical reasons behind how they act. But I don't know—they're so ridiculous, it's almost like somebody created them just to be villains in a movie or book. Either way, I started avoiding the island last year. There isn't much there, anyway."

"You've been . . . there?" Evey asked.

"Yea. My parents took me when I was little. It's a jungle on there."

Evey nodded, remembering the tree roots she stumbled on.

"So, what were you doing hanging around the island?" Archer asked.

Evey thought about her grandma's crystal, still tucked under her life vest. She looked at Archer, unsure whether she wanted to reveal it. His wide smile and big eyes seemed to ask what she was waiting for. *Stop being so suspicious,* Evey thought. *He did just save me.*

Evey took the crystal out from under her vest and held it for Archer to see. "Trying to . . . to learn about . . . this," she said.

"Whoa, that's awesome!" Archer paddled his kayak closer to Evey's for a better look. "Is it real?"

Evey nodded. "It's my grandma's. She died before I . . . was born. She . . . found it by . . . the island. I was . . . looking for more."

"Did you find any?" Archer asked.

Evey shook her head no.

"Do you know anything else about it?"

"Not much," Evey said. "I forgot I even . . . had it until last night. I was trying to leap—I mean . . . sleep, and . . . the moonlight was . . . reflecting off it. It looked like . . . glowing. I think I . . . was . . . dreaming."

Archer squinted as he looked at the crystal. "Dreaming or not, I'd be careful wearing that thing around your neck. In movies, old artifacts like that are always haunted."

Evey shrugged. *I would like to say that's ridiculous,* she thought, *but part of me thinks he could be right.*

"I'm just saying," Archer continued, "you might bring a mummy back to life with that thing. Or worse—zombies."

Evey laughed as she continued paddling. *Should I tell him about my dream—memory—whatever it was,* she wondered. *Does it make me sound crazy? Although, it might actually be better to be known as the girl who hallucinates than the girl who can't talk.*

Evey looked at Archer again. A big smile still covered his face. She took a deep breath. "The glowing is only the . . . start," she said.

Evey told Archer about the foggy island, the shadowy man, the howling, and the bright light she thought came from a lighthouse. Archer listened closely. By the time Evey finished, the two had reached her grandpa's dock.

"That is literally the coolest thing anybody has ever told me," Archer said. "I wish I had dreams like that. Mine are usually about my sisters beating me in badminton."

"It didn't . . . feel like a dream," Evey said.

"It sounds more like a vision to me. Maybe you're actually some kind of witch."

Evey rolled her eyes.

"All seriousness, Evey," Archer continued, "we need to find out more about that crystal. Assuming it doesn't turn you into a zombie, it probably has a cool story behind it."

"If you know . . . where to . . . start. My idea ran into a dead end by . . . that . . . island."

"Yea, I guess we don't want to go back there. Wait—I got it!" Archer clapped his hands together. "Let's take it to the museum!"

Evey raised her eyebrow.

Archer looked confused. "The Door County Historical Museum. You've never been there?"

Evey shook her head no.

"Seriously? It's in Apple Bay, like five minutes away."

Evey shrugged.

"My parents have taken me a few times," Archer said. "They're both teachers and always drag me to those things. I remember it being really boring. Actually, I don't even like history now that I think about it, but that's because there's usually nothing about haunted crystals and . . ."

What is he talking about now? Evey thought. She nodded as she struggled to keep up with Archer's rambling.

"Anyway," Archer continued, "maybe we can find something there."

"You mean . . . go today?" Evey asked.

"Sure! I'm free. Just come get me whenever you can go. I bet we can find something—wait, I almost forgot. My family is going to the state park today. What about visiting the museum tomorrow?"

Evey frowned. "I'm going . . . home."

"Oh, that stinks. I'm here most of the summer, so you can stop by if you come back. I'm in the ugly yellow house, a few down from you."

Evey nodded as she pulled her kayak into the dock. "We usually come back over the . . . Fourth of July."

"I'll be here," Archer said. He started turning his kayak around.

"Hey, Archer," Evey said. Archer stopped paddling and looked at her. "Tanks," she said. "I mean . . ."

"Your welcome!" Archer shouted. "Just make sure that crystal doesn't end the world before I see you again!"

Evey nodded. As Archer paddled away, she looked at her grandma's crystal. *Let's see if Grandpa knows more about you,* she thought.

CHAPTER 6

Howie pulled at his leash while Evey dragged the kayak out of the water. "Sorry, Howie," she said as she untied the leash. He gave her hand a few licks, then found a spot in the grass to stretch out.

Evey lugged the kayak back to the shed and turned it upside down to dry off. Hoping her grandpa was still asleep, she quietly put the paddle and life vest in the shed, then jogged to the house with Howie at her side. She opened the porch door and tiptoed in.

"Where were you?" Alex said loudly, making Evey jump.

"Shush!" she said with her finger to her mouth. "Kayaking."

"You kayaked alone?" Alex asked. "You're not allowed to do that."

Evey rolled her eyes. "I was . . . with a . . . friend."

"You have friends up here? Who?"

"He lives—"

"He?" Alex interrupted. "You have a boyfriend now?"

Evey grabbed her grandpa's fishing hat from a hook on the wall and shoved it over Alex's head, covering his face. "Don't tell anybody," Evey said. "I'll pack your . . . suitcase." She took the hat off. "Deal?"

"Fine," Alex said. He glared at her as he rubbed his short, blond hair.

Evey walked to the kitchen. She forgot to eat or drink anything before she left the house. Her throat felt scratchy, and her stomach rumbled with hunger pains. She poured herself a glass of water and made a bowl of cereal. She took a seat on the couch next to Alex as he drew in his sketchbook. Even though her cousin was a year younger than Evey, people often mistook them for twins as they looked very similar except for their hair.

"Where is . . . everybody?" Evey asked after swallowing a spoonful of cereal.

"My parents went golfing," Alex said. "Your parents are on a bike ride, and Grandpa is still in bed."

At the mention of Grandpa, Howie trotted down the hallway and pushed his nose into the back bedroom. A few minutes later, Grandpa staggered to the kitchen wearing his pajamas and eyeglasses. Howie followed right behind. "Morning," Grandpa mumbled with a groggy voice.

Evey turned, but only saw the back of Grandpa's head as he dug around the refrigerator. She noticed the small, gray spot in his hair. Despite nearing seventy years old, Grandpa's hair was almost entirely brown.

Is his hair really that color, or does he dye it and always miss that spot? Evey wondered.

Grandpa came out of the kitchen with a large glass of almond milk and surveyed the view from the porch. "I haven't seen the lake this smooth in a while," he said. "The calm came after the storm, this time."

"Torm—I mean . . . storm?" Evey asked.

32

"Yep, a big storm blew in after you went to bed. We were in the garage playing some ping-pong for the Championship. I'm surprised it didn't wake you up."

"Who won?" Alex asked.

Grandpa puffed his chest. "I won both of my matches last night, so I'm in the final game on the Fourth of July. Same in foosball."

"Do you really think you can win the Championship this year, Grandpa?" Alex asked. "My dad's been talking about a three-peat for months."

"The turtle hat is as good as mine!" Grandpa said as he wiped milk from his chin.

Evey normally paid attention to the Championship—her family's yearly competition to see who would keep their cherished turtle hat for the next year. This time, she ignored Grandpa and Alex as she wondered if the real storm was related to her dream.

"What are you thinking about?" Grandpa asked Evey.

"I . . . had a dream that it torm I mean . . . stormed," she said while thinking about the island. "Any chance you . . . heard . . . howling, last night?"

"No, why? Did you dream that too?"

Evey shook her head yes.

"It was probably Howie," Alex said. "Remember, before dinner yesterday, Howie was howling while my dad was playing piano."

Evey nodded. *Thank goodness*, she thought. *Add a point to the 'I don't need my head examined' side.*

"Why does Howie do that, Grandpa?" Alex asked.

"I'm not really sure," Grandpa said. "He started it after your grandma died. Some piano notes must remind him of the stuff she used to play."

Evey took the crystal necklace out from under her shirt. "Speaking of Grandma, my dad said she . . . found . . . this in the lake. Do you . . . know more?"

"Is that why you went kayaking?" Alex asked.

Evey glared at Alex.

"You went kayaking by yourself?" Grandpa asked. "Are you supposed to do that?"

Evey rolled her eyes.

"She wasn't alone," Alex said. "She was with her new boyfriend."

Evey slapped Alex's sketchbook, knocking it to the ground.

"Hey!" he said. "I'm designing a new condo for my Lego town. And besides, I'm only trying to help."

Grandpa smiled. "Don't worry. I won't tell anybody. Neither will Alex, right?"

"Whatever," Alex grumbled as he picked up his book.

"Do you . . . know more?" Evey asked again as she pointed to the crystal.

Grandpa rubbed his chin. "Let me take a look at it." Evey handed the crystal over. "Hmm," Grandpa said as he inspected it. "I remember she found it right before she got sick. She liked the thing so much that I attached the string so she could wear it as a necklace. After that, she took it to a jeweler. They said it looks like a rare dolomite crystal."

Evey raised her eyebrow.

"Dolomite is a type of bedrock," Grandpa said.

Evey raised her other eyebrow.

"I wish you never inherited that," Grandpa said. "Your dad used to always do that to me."

Evey shrugged.

"Anyway," Grandpa continued, "bedrock just refers to what's below the dirt. In Door County, it's mostly dolomite or limestone. Usually, it just looks like a rock, but sometimes it comes in a crystal form like this. Although, in Door County the crystals are usually a clear color."

"How do you know all of that?" Alex asked.

"I read it in a geology book," Grandpa said.

"Did Grandma . . . find anything else?" Evey asked.

"If I remember right, she thought it had something to do with an old legend—about a pirate."

"Pirates? Like, argh?" Alex said. "That doesn't make any sense."

"It sounds goofy, right?" Grandpa said. "I don't remember the details, unfortunately. I do know once Grandma got sick, she kept talking about wanting her grandchild to have the crystal, even though neither of you were born yet. She had . . ."

Evey sunk into the couch cushion and thought about what Grandpa said. *A pirate—that makes perfect sense actually. It's scary how much that makes sense. Mr. Shadow from last night looked like a pirate. Is Archer right? Was that some kind of vision? Either way, give a point to the 'I do need my head examined' side.*

"Did Grandma make any notes about the thing?" Alex asked Grandpa.

"She probably did!" Grandpa said. "Your grandma had an old book where she kept all kinds of notes about Door

County—parks, restaurants, her garden, and whatnot. If she found anything, I'm sure it will be in there. Wait here."

Grandpa went to his room. Evey heard him rummaging through the closet.

"You're welcome," Alex said.

Evey faked a smile.

A minute later, Grandpa returned with a large box and set it on the kitchen table. He wiped off the dust and opened it. "Wow, I didn't know this stuff was in here," he said.

"What?" Evey asked as she walked from the porch to the kitchen.

Grandpa pulled out a large photo album. "If I remember right, this is her first-year album. We were up here a bunch the first year after we bought this place. She took so many pictures."

"When was that?" Alex asked as he walked over to the table.

"About twenty-five years ago. Your dads were still teenagers."

Evey flipped through the album. She saw pictures of her dad, uncle, and grandparents. She also recognized some other family members, including her great-grandparents. The pictures showed her family swimming in the lake, playing badminton and ping-pong, roasting marshmallows, mini-golfing, building sand castles, fishing, and more.

Alex pointed to a picture of a soaking wet Grandpa holding a putter. "What's with that one, Grandpa?" he asked.

"Nothing important," Grandpa mumbled as he quickly flipped the page. The last picture in the book showed him and Evey's grandma lying in a hammock.

"You two look so . . . young," Evey said.

"We were only in our forties. That's about the same age your parents are now." Grandpa turned to a previous page and pointed to a picture of Evey's parents. "See your parents—they look like kids."

Evey inspected the picture. It showed her mom and dad smiling in a restaurant booth with large sundaes in front of them.

"Is that Chester's?" Alex asked.

"Yep, why? You want some ice cream?" Grandpa asked with a big smile.

"Yes!" Alex said. "Although, we have to wait for my dad."

Evey chuckled. *Ice cream for breakfast. Like grandfather, like father, like son*, she thought.

Grandpa closed the photo album and put his arms around Evey and Alex. "I'm glad we found this," he said. "Lots of good memories. Come on, let's keep digging to see if your grandma's notes are in here."

The three looked back in the box. Grandpa moved some items around and pulled out a large, worn notebook. "This is what we're looking for," he said as he set it on the table.

Grandpa started to open the notebook, but a strong gust of wind blew through the porch and into the kitchen. Loose pages blew out of the book and fluttered in the air. Evey and Alex chased after them while Grandpa closed the porch windows.

"That was weird," Grandpa said. "If I didn't know any better, I'd think we're in a scary movie."

Evey froze when she remembered what Archer said about the crystal being haunted. *Maybe I should just put the crystal away and go back to bed,* she thought. *Maybe have a normal last day of vacation—some swimming, ice cream—*

"Hey, you okay?" Grandpa asked as he waved his hand in front of Evey. "You look paler than usual."

Evey rolled her eyes. "I'm . . . fine," she mumbled. She looked at her arms. *And I do have somewhat of a tan,* she thought.

"Okay," Grandpa said. He walked to the kitchen. "I need to take care of Howie and make myself something to eat. Why don't you two see what you can find in your grandma's notes."

Evey and Alex took the notebook to the porch and set it on the table. They sat next to each other on the couch and started reviewing the pages.

The notebook was organized into sections. The first contained entries about the changes Evey's grandma wanted to make to the house. The second covered gardening. The third detailed places to visit in Door County. Evey noticed familiar spots her family often went to including Chester's, Pirate's Park Mini-Golf, the Scottish Inn Restaurant, Cave Falls Park, and Pancake Harbor Beach.

"Here," Evey said as she flipped to the fourth section. "Kayaking notes." She found a worn map tucked into the page. She carefully unfolded it.

"What's that?" Alex asked.

"A map of Door County," Evey said as she brought the map closer to her face. "I think Grandma . . . circled places she wanted to kayak—Turtle Lake, East Bay, Eagle Island, Whitney Lake."

"How do you know all those places?" Alex asked.

"Because I've . . . seen a map of Door County."

"You mean like a million times."

Evey rolled her eyes.

"Don't roll your eyes at me, Evey. Seriously, I've never met anybody who stares at maps like you."

Evey felt her jaw stiffen as she tried to think of a response. She started studying maps as a little kid. Something about them helped her relax. "I like . . . to know dare tings are," she said as she tossed the map at Alex's face.

"I still say you're weird," he said.

"Me? You're drawing a Lego . . . condo. Shouldn't you build a . . . spaceship?"

"Spaceships—really, Evey?" Alex said as he put his hands on his hips. "I'm not a baby. My Legos are sophisticated models, not toys."

Evey rolled her eyes again and turned back to the notebook. The next few pages included entries about her grandma's first few kayaking trips in Turtle Lake. They covered deep and shallow spots, where she found turtles, the types of birds and ducks she saw, and the best places to view the sunrise. Evey stopped on a page with a drawing of the crystal.

"Is that the crystal?" Alex asked.

Evey nodded, then took the real crystal off and laid it next to the picture. The drawing matched the red shade and jagged texture.

"What did Grandma write about it?" Alex asked.

Evey read the notes under the drawing:

> Found this crystal in the lake near the island this morning. Was out with Howie on one of my usual trips. Was poking around the north side of the island, looking

for cool rocks and shells. On the way back home, saw bright reflection in water, dove in and found crystal partially buried under a rock.

Evey stared motionless at the page while she replayed her vision of grabbing the crystal in the lake. *My vision by the island—am I seeing Grandma's memories?* she thought. *That's impossible. Maybe I've just read this before. That's it, right? No, I've never seen this notebook. Ugh! What is going on with—*

Alex shook Evey.

"What!" she yelled.

"Just making sure you're alive," Alex said. "You look like you're going to pass out."

"I was just tinking—I mean . . . thinking."

"You should get your head checked when you go home. You seem off."

Evey gently threw a pillow at Alex's face. *Tell me about it,* she thought.

Alex laughed. "What else does the notebook say?"

Evey read the next entry:

Went to the library to research. Only thing about crystals I found was a reference to an old pirate legend in Door County (weird, right?). Planning on taking the crystal to the Door County Historical Museum to see if they can give me more info.

"Seriously," Alex said, "how were there possibly pirates in Door County?"

Evey shrugged. *Maybe they liked vacationing here like us Illinois people do*, she thought. She kept reading:

> Made it to the museum today. A nice professor was able to help. After talking with her, I'm convinced the crystal has something to do with "The Door County Pirate." Apparently, he was real. He raided ships in Lake Michigan in the 1850s. Can't believe there was a pirate around here. The tale says he acquired quite a treasure, including crystals. Nobody ever found it. The only known artifact from him is a letter to some lady named Evelyn. Apparently, the Navy intercepted it before it reached her.

Alex looked at Evey. "Evelyn—same as you—that's an interesting coincidence. I guess you get that with an old-fashioned name."

Evey tried to look calm despite feeling woozy. *The way today is going,* she thought, *if my name wasn't old-fashioned, I might have a panic attack.*

"I still don't believe that thing is actually pirate treasure," Alex said. "Let me take a look at it."

Evey handed the crystal to Alex. As he inspected it, she quietly read the next section:

> I wouldn't think much of this pirate story, but I've been having weird dreams lately. They don't feel like dreams though. I find myself on an island surrounded by tall grass. A bright light keeps circling overhead. And there's a man. I can only see his outline, but with his hat, coat, and boots, he looks like a pirate to me. He tries to

talk to me, but I can't remember much. It's usually something about "sunrise." I thought the light might be a lighthouse, but then again, I have lighthouse pictures all over the place. So, maybe it's just a sign that I need to stop collecting them. Jokes aside, I wish I could make sense of this.

Evey leaned back into the sofa with her mouth wide open. *This is starting to feel scary,* she thought. *Grandma and I apparently had the same dream—or vision—how is that even possible? She wrote this years ago. And didn't Mr. Shadow say he saw someone else with the crystal who looked like—*

Another gust of wind blew into the porch, flipping the notebook's pages. Loose papers flew around the room.

"Grandpa missed a window!" Alex yelled as he scrambled to close the last open window.

When the wind stopped, the journal settled on a page with a large drawing. Evey cautiously inspected it. It showed a shadowy man with a long coat, boots, and a tricorn hat.

That picture, Evey thought, *which Grandma drew years ago, definitely looks like Mr. Shadow—who I saw in a dream, last night.* Evey rubbed her temples. *Maybe Archer is right—this crystal is haunted!*

"What's all the noise in here?" Grandpa said as he poked his head into the porch. Alex told him about the wind gust as he picked up the scattered pages.

"Find something in there, Evey?" Grandpa waved his hand in front of her face. "Hey, you okay?"

"I don't think so," Alex said as he pointed to Evey's head. Evey pushed Alex away. "I'm . . . fine."

"You sure?" Grandpa said. "You look really pale again."

Evey tilted her head and sighed.

"Well?" Grandpa said.

"Uh . . ." Evey paused, hesitant to discuss the details of her vision. Alex and Grandpa were both logical types who did not believe in supernatural things. "I . . . think I need . . . to explore the lake," she said.

Grandpa smiled. "You know, I thought of something while I was eating that might help you with that. Let's go for a ride."

CHAPTER 7

Grandpa drove Evey to a storage facility about ten minutes away. Alex's parents returned before they left, so Alex stayed behind to help his mom in the garden. At the end of the short drive, Evey and Grandpa pulled into a parking lot in front of a large, gray warehouse. Several boats sat scattered around the property. Evey recognized the place as where Grandpa stored his pontoon boat in the winter.

"Why are we . . . here?" Evey asked.

"You'll see," Grandpa said with a wink.

Grandpa parked his truck, and the two walked into a small office in the front of the warehouse. A tall, stocky man with a white mustache stood behind a desk.

"How's it going, Will?" Grandpa asked. He shook the man's hand.

"Good," Will said. "What are you doing here in summer? You're not supposed to drop your boat off for a few months. Any problems with it?"

"Nope, it's great. My son and I have been fishing almost every morning." Grandpa put his arm around Evey. "Even got this one out a few times."

Will looked at Evey. "Did you catch anything?" he asked.

Evey shook her head no, remembering the driftwood she reeled in a few days earlier.

"That's too bad," Will said. "In that case, what can I do for you two?"

"I'm finally ready to take my other boat home," Grandpa said.

"No kidding! It's funny you mention it. I forgot about that old thing, but just the other day I stumbled across it while searching for a lost tool. It looks the same as when you left it."

Grandpa made a squeamish face. "That bad, huh?"

"I've seen worse," Will said. "I'm sure you can fix it up. Follow me."

The three left the office and walked to a smaller shed at the back of the property. Will opened the door and turned on a light.

Yikes, Evey thought. *I think everything in here is older than Grandpa.* Rusted boat and engine parts littered every corner. She also saw some busted bicycles and an old car missing its hood and wheels.

Will led Evey and Grandpa through a winding maze of old equipment until they reached a dusty tarp covering something big. Grandpa pulled the tarp off, sending the dust flying in the air. Evey sneezed. After wiping her nose and eyes, she looked down at a small sailboat—a catamaran with two hulls. Two long beams held the hulls together. A torn-up trampoline stretched across the gap between them. Evey judged the boat was about thirteen feet long.

"Here it is," Will said. "It's been what, ten years since you left this here?"

"Something like that," Grandpa said. "So, Evey, would you like to go sailing on Turtle Lake?"

Evey felt too excited to put any words together. She squeezed her fingers instead. Ever since her family took a sail cruise in Lake Michigan a few years prior, she hoped they would one day buy a sailboat.

"Evey?" Grandpa said.

She nodded, still feeling too overwhelmed to open her mouth. While Grandpa continued talking with Will, Evey walked around the boat. She ran her hand across one of the hulls. It felt dented, and she noticed a few small cracks. The color looked as if it was originally white, but dirt and age turned it to a brownish yellow. The mast sat next to the boat in two pieces. Evey thought it would stand twenty feet tall when put together.

"What do you think?" Grandpa asked.

Evey rubbed her jaw. "Awesome," she said. "When can we get it . . . in . . . water?"

"Let's worry about getting it to the house, first."

Will and Grandpa carried the boat outside. Will loaned Grandpa a trailer. They hooked it up to the truck, then mounted the boat on it. Grandpa and Evey thanked Will, then started the drive back to the house.

"How long . . . you had this boat?" Evey asked.

"Your grandma bought it not long before you were born," Grandpa said. "She liked kayaking, but she wanted something we could take on longer trips. But we never got around to fixing it up once she got sick."

"Oh," Evey said. "Why did you put it in . . . storage?"

"The garage was too crowded and I didn't want to leave it outside. And I didn't want to get rid of it. I hoped your dad, uncle, or one of you kids would use it."

"Do you know how to ail . . . sail, I mean?"

"I know enough to get you started."

Evey smiled. "Can we go today?"

"Not so fast," Grandpa said. "Remember, I said we never got around to fixing it up. We didn't want to buy an expensive, new boat. Grandma found this one in Pancake Harbor for just a few hundred dollars."

"How much . . . work does it need?"

"It needs a good cleaning, first. And you saw the dents. We need to take care of those. And replace the trampoline over the hulls. Then give it a fresh coat of paint. And fix the rigging. And it needs sails."

Evey bit her lip. "Sounds . . . expensive. Can I—"

"Don't worry about it, Evey," Grandpa cut in. "Technically, it's my boat, so I'll take care of it."

"Tanks, Grandpa," Evey said. "I can help . . . fix it."

"I appreciate the offer, but remember, you're leaving tomorrow."

All the excitement from the morning had made Evey forget about going home. She frowned as she thought about how much she wanted to work on the boat and research the crystal.

Grandpa put his hand on Evey's shoulder. "Don't worry. You'll be back in a few weeks. I'll see if I can get the boat ready for the Fourth."

Evey nodded and forced a small smile. "Where did you learn how to . . . fix boats?"

"I've read some boating books," Grandpa said with a wink. "Now that I think of it, why don't we stop at the Adventure Center to see if they have anything we can use. It may take a while to get sails in the right size, so we should order them now."

Grandpa turned the truck around and headed across the Door County peninsula until they reached the Adventure Center in Pancake Harbor. Evey thought the dark brown building looked like an old log cabin. Several kayaks hung behind a huge triangular shaped window over the front door. Inside, large log beams crossed the ceiling. A chandelier made of wooden wheels hung from one of the logs.

"Over there," Grandpa said, pointing to the left side of the room.

The two walked past the kayaks and found a series of large posters showing different types of boats that the store sold. Shelves along the wall displayed various accessories including paddles and life vests. Evey saw two small sails at the end of the shelves.

"I see you found the sails," Grandpa said. "These look nice, but we need something a lot bigger for the mainsail. Plus, we need a jib."

Evey raised her eyebrow.

"We'll have to work on your sailing vocab," Grandpa said. "The jib is a small sail on the front of the boat. It helps keep the boat steady. Here, let's look at this." He found a catalog and started flipping through the pages. "I think they have what we need, but we may have to order it. See if you can find somebody to help us."

Evey walked to the front desk and found an employee. She followed Evey to the sailboat section. "Hi," the employee said when she reached Grandpa. "I hear you need help finding some sails."

"Yep," Grandpa said. "We have a small catamaran that needs a mainsail and a jib. Here are the dimensions of the boat and mast. Do you have anything in stock we can use or will we have to order some?"

The employee looked at the sizes listed on Grandpa's note. "We don't keep anything of that size here, so we'll have to order them. I can check to see how long it'll take. All the designs are in that book if you want to pick one out."

"Thanks," Grandpa said as the woman returned to the sales desk. He turned back to the book. "Do you like any of these, Evey?"

Evey was staring at one of the display sails on the wall. The bottom of the sail was yellow and orange, but it changed to shades of red, pink, and purple toward the top.

"Looks like you picked one already," Grandpa said. "Quite colorful."

Evey snapped out of her daze. "This one— looks like a . . . sunrise."

Grandpa looked at the sail again. "You're right, it does. Pretty neat."

The two walked to the sales desk. "Did you pick one?" the employee asked.

Evey pointed to the sail on the wall. "Can we get the . . . reddish one in the two . . . sizes we need?"

"Certainly! We should be able to get them to you in a few weeks. Does that work?"

Grandpa nodded. "We don't need them until the Fourth, so that should be fine." He paid for the order and the two left the store. "Since we're already out," he said, "let's head to the hardware store and pick up the rest of the supplies we need. What do you think about paint colors? We could add some designs to the hull. You don't have to stick with all white. Any thoughts, Evey?"

"Red," she said with a smile.

CHAPTER 8

Evey's family, including Howie, walked to Coyote Grill for dinner that night. The small restaurant and its dog-friendly patio sat on the shore of Turtle Lake, next to the bridge on the northern end.

A life-size, wooden sculpture of a howling coyote stood outside the front door. Alex patted the coyote's head as he usually did. Evey did the same, but flinched as she flashbacked to the howling in her vision.

"What was that?" Alex asked.

"Uh . . . just a . . . a bug," Evey replied.

"Must have been a big bug. You almost fell over."

Howie sniffed the statue.

"Howie, guard dog!" Alex said.

Howie snarled and barked relentlessly at the statue.

"Oh, knock it off," Grandpa said as he grabbed Howie and shook a finger at Alex.

"I'm just practicing his tricks," Alex said.

Evey rolled her eyes as Alex laughed. Once the family entered the restaurant, the hostess led them to a large table on the patio. Evey took a seat between her dad and Alex.

"Mom, can I go inside to play *Galaga*?" Alex asked.

"What do you want to eat?" Evey's aunt replied.

"My usual, please."

"Alright. Evey, why don't you go with?"

Grandpa leaned back in his chair and put his hands behind his head. "Still trying to beat my record," he said. "Keep dreaming, kids. Not even your dads can touch me."

Evey's dad laughed. "Nobody cares about the one video game you're good at. Besides, you only brag about *Galaga* because you can't beat us in foosball, anymore."

"Or ping-pong," Evey's uncle added.

"Oh, whatever," Grandpa said as he waved his hands back-and-forth. "Just because I'm in a little drought doesn't mean anything. And besides, I've got my new glasses this time. I just couldn't see good enough the last few years."

"Are those glasses going to help you fish better?" Evey's uncle said. He and Evey's dad both laughed.

As Evey's dad, uncle, and grandpa continued bickering, her mom leaned over and excused her from the table. She followed Alex inside the restaurant and past the long, wooden bar to the old arcade game *Galaga*.

Alex dropped a few quarters in the machine. Evey watched as he rammed the joystick to move his starfighter across the screen. Insect-looking alien ships massed together and moved down to attack. Alex frantically dodged them while firing his weapons. As usual, he let out a loud "Yes!" upon beating the first level. "Grandpa's record is going down," he said.

You have about a hundred levels to go, Evey thought. As Alex continued, her eyes wandered around the room. She noticed a painting of a howling coyote on a nearby wall. She had seen it before, but never noticed the background. The coyote stood on a beach, in between the water and tall grass.

Evey walked over to take a closer look. *That looks just like my vision,* she thought. *That's so—*

"Something fascinating about that picture?" asked a person behind Evey.

Evey turned around to see a waitress holding a tray of empty plates. "Uh . . ." Evey mumbled. "Is that . . . Turtle Lake?"

"It is," the waitress replied. "The coyote in the picture is on the island."

"There aren't really coyotes dare—I mean . . . there, right?"

The waitress pointed to a poster hanging a few feet away from the painting. "According to the legend there are, or used to be."

Evey raised her eyebrow.

"You've never heard of the legend?" the waitress asked. "That's what this place is named after. Check it out."

Evey nodded as the waitress carried the tray into the kitchen. She walked to the poster and read:

The Coyote Island Legend

French fur traders were the first Europeans to pass through Door County. While trading with Native Americans, they were warned of packs of aggressive coyotes surrounding the area now known as Turtle Lake. Once American and European settlers began logging the nearby woods, tales of attacks by wolf-sized coyotes quickly spread. All attempts to catch or kill the coyotes failed.

During a particularly harsh winter in the middle of the nineteenth century, the coyotes crossed the frozen lake to find food on the island. After a few weeks, a quick thaw broke up the ice and stranded them. Their food quickly dwindled, and by spring the coyotes found themselves starving. Desperate, one tried to swim back to shore, but drowned in the cold water. For the next two weeks, the remaining coyotes howled every night until they too died of starvation.

After several years of quiet, settlers began noticing the distinct howling of the coyotes coming from the island once again. In the years that followed, those who traveled there reported being chased off by growling animals. While no pictures or videos of the coyotes exist, many say you can still hear their howls.

Evey took a step back from the poster. Her mind returned to the howling in her vision. *I'm trying to convince myself that this crystal stuff is cool and not scary, but I don't think it's working*, she thought. She pulled the crystal out from under her shirt and rubbed it. *What is this thing?*

"What do you think?" the waitress asked from the bar.

Evey put the crystal back under her shirt. "Have you . . . heard the coyotes?" she asked.

"Sure. They howl pretty often, but I don't think they're on the island. They're probably on the north side of the lake. It's pretty wooded up there. One time, though, some friends and I were on a boat late at night and we anchored right next to the island. I heard some loud howls that night. That was a long time ago, though."

"Stuck at level four again!" Alex yelled. "How does Grandpa beat this? He has to have some kind of trick."

Evey glanced at the poster again, then walked back to the game and put a few quarters in. She took a turn and made it to level five. The two then returned to the table a few minutes before dinner arrived.

Evey ate her usual pan-fried perch with fries. She thought about the trip home the next day as she ate her food. She felt disappointed about leaving the sailboat and not being able to find out more about the crystal. She tried to think of fun things to do at home to cheer herself up, but struggled to come up with much. The first part of summer was mostly quiet for Evey. Her parents both worked, so she spent most of her time reading, drawing maps, and running.

If this crystal's secret is real, Evey thought, *what if I can find it? That might make my parents stop focusing on how I talk, for once.* Evey swallowed a bite of fish. *Wait a minute,* she thought, *do I have to go home? Speech camp is in July, and cross country practice doesn't start until August.*

Evey had never stayed at Grandpa's lake house without her parents. *Dad always says Grandpa loves having family up here,* she thought. *If I can stay for a few weeks, I can help fix the boat, explore the lake, and hopefully figure out this mystery. And it would be nice to take a break from my parents pointing out every time I say something stupid.*

Evey tried to anticipate her parents' response. *They do always want me to act independent,* she thought. She took another bite of fish as she thought about the best way to ask them. *Dad was so excited to give me the crystal last year. If I finish what Grandma started, maybe they'll feel—*

"Evey," her mom said, "you look really focused on something. What are you thinking about?"

Evey froze. *How does Mom always do that?* she thought. *Quick, say something!* Evey slowly finished chewing a bite of fish, swallowed, and took a sip of water. By now, everybody at the table stared at her. "Uh . . ." she mumbled.

"Spit it out," Alex said.

Evey's jaw tensed up as she tried to put a response together. After another moment of silence, her family started talking amongst themselves again. Relieved, Evey let out a large sigh and took another bite of her fish.

"What is it?" her dad asked quietly. "Your cheeks are red. It's making your Triforce pop."

Evey rolled her eyes. Her dad often referred to the three moles on her left cheek as the "Triforce"—a sacred artifact from an old video game. The three moles outlined a triangle, and when her cheeks turned red, it seemed to highlight them.

"You can tell me," Evey's dad said.

Evey rubbed her jaw. "I wanted to . . . ask if I can tay—no, I mean . . ."

"Put your thoughts together before you talk, like your exercises."

Evey ground her teeth. *Why do you always have to point it out?* she thought. She took a deep breath. "Stay—can I . . . stay with Grandpa?"

"Did you say stay with Grandpa?"

Evey nodded.

"You mean until the Fourth?" her dad asked.

Evey nodded again.

"That's surprising to hear. Why do you want to stay?"

Evey told a brief version of the day's events, leaving out the vision and solo trip in the kayak. She emphasized wanting to research her grandma's crystal and work on the sailboat.

"Pirates in Door County," her dad said. "That seems unlikely, but I'm certainly not one to get in the way of a pirate adventure. Next thing you know you'll be Geena Davis from *Cutthroat Island*."

Evey raised her eyebrow.

"It's an amazing pirate movie from the nineties," her dad said.

Evey shrugged.

"It got terrible reviews and bankrupted a studio, but I still think it's great. We should watch it sometime."

Evey tried to nod politely. She knew many of her dad's 1990s references, but this one escaped her. Her dad turned to her mom and relayed Evey's request to stay with Grandpa. Evey could tell from their eyes and facial expressions that they were discussing it without talking. She could make out that they were both enthused, but a little worried.

Evey's dad turned back to her. "I think it's up to your grandpa." He looked at Grandpa across the table. "Hey, Dad, can Evey stay up here until the Fourth of July?"

Grandpa, who was leaning his chair back on its rear legs, nearly fell over. "Seriously?" he said.

Evey shook her head yes.

"That would be great! I could use the help around here. And we can work on the boat together."

Evey could not contain the large smile on her face. She squeezed her fingers. "Tanks," she whispered to her parents.

The waitress returned with a large cherry pie. Evey eagerly ate her dessert while planning a trip to the museum with Archer the next day.

A glowing crystal, a pirate, a lighthouse, a secret, and coyotes, Evey thought. *Hopefully, I can figure out how all of these weird things fit together.*

CHAPTER 9

Howie was the only one to greet Evey the next morning when she walked into the living room. She noticed a steady rain falling outside, so she let him out on his own. He found a spot in the grass to relieve himself, then quickly ran back to the porch door. She let him in and dried him off, then headed to the kitchen. She made a bowl of cereal to eat while reviewing her grandma's notes, then put the notebook and some snacks in her backpack.

Evey tried to pass the rest of the morning by helping her family pack. Before leaving, her mom ran through a list of rules they agreed to. Evey was to wash the dishes, take out the garbage, and help clean the house. Plus, she was to take sailing lessons so that she would know how to safely handle the sailboat.

"And one last thing," her mom said. "Don't forget your speech exercises while you're up here."

There it is, Evey thought as she stopped herself from rolling her eyes. *I've been doing them my whole life. It's kind of like asking me not to forget to sleep at this point. I think it's safe to say I—*

"Evey," her mom loudly said. "Are you okay?"

"Uh . . . yea," Evey said.

After a round of hugs and goodbyes, Evey's parents started their drive home. Evey ran back inside and flipped through a tourism magazine to find the museum's phone number.

"When is Grandpa getting internet?" Evey mumbled as she flipped through the pages.

"Never," Evey's aunt said with a smile. "We've been bugging him about it for years."

Evey found the phone number and called the museum. A recording answered and stated that the museum opened at ten. *Perfect!* she thought. *Just enough time to get Archer and bike to town.* She filled a water bottle, grabbed her backpack, and started digging through the closet for a raincoat.

"Are you going out in this weather?" Evey's aunt asked as she motioned to the window.

Evey backed out of the closet and shook her head yes.

"Why don't you wait for Grandpa. I'm sure he can drive you."

Evey raised her eyebrow. Grandpa had briefly come out to say goodbye to her parents, but then yawned and went back to his room.

"I guess that might be a while," Evey's aunt said. They both laughed. "I'll let him know where you are. Just bring your phone so you can call him if it starts to thunder."

Evey ran to her room and grabbed her phone. "Where are you going?" Alex asked.

"Museum," Evey replied.

"Did you forget our deal?" Alex motioned to his open suitcase and messy pile of clothes.

Evey rolled her eyes. She tossed Alex's clothes into the suitcase as quickly as possible.

"It's not going to fit if you throw everything in like that!" Alex protested.

Evey pressed the top of the suitcase down, but she could not close the zipper.

"See," Alex said. "Maybe try folding everything, nicely."

Evey smirked and grabbed Alex's legs. She pulled him off the bed.

"Hey!" he yelled as he fell on the suitcase with a loud thud.

Evey ignored his mumbling while she squeezed the zipper around the suitcase until it shut. She waved and ran out of the room before Alex could retaliate. She said goodbye to her aunt and uncle, then left the house and jogged to the garage.

Grandpa only parked vehicles in the garage during the winter. In the summer, it housed a ping-pong table, foosball table, and air-hockey table. A large assortment of beach toys, water guns, and rafts littered one corner. A collection of old and newer bikes filled another.

Evey took her grandma's old, red nine-speed, put on a helmet, and pedaled down the driveway to the road. The bike's tires made a zipping sound as they rolled through the puddles covering the road. A few houses down, she recognized Archer's family's place from its yellow paint and crooked-looking roof. She rode down the driveway and set her bike by the front door. She rang the doorbell and waited.

A woman opened the door and gave Evey a confused expression. Judging by her looks, Evey figured she was Archer's mom. "Is Archer here?" Evey asked.

"Yes," the woman said. "Would you be Evey by any chance?"

Evey shook her head yes.

"Come on in out of the rain, then." The woman turned toward the back of the house. "Archer, your friend Evey's here!" she yelled. She turned back to Evey. "I'm Archer's mom, Katie. It's nice to meet you." Evey smiled as she and Archer's mom shook hands.

"Evey, what are you doing here?" Archer asked when he reached the foyer. "I thought you were going home today."

Evey told Archer how her parents agreed to let her stay with Grandpa. "Do you . . . still want to go to the . . . museum?" she asked.

Archer's mom cut in before he could answer. "You want to bike there in this weather?"

"Mom, didn't you hear Evey?" Archer said. "The museum! History! Old stuff! You should be happy. I'm following in your footsteps."

"Oh, I guess. Speaking of that, since when do you want to go to the museum?"

"Super-secret stuff. I probably shouldn't tell you. You might turn into a pirate zombie."

Archer's mom laughed. "Okay, but it still looks pretty bad out."

"You always say there is no such thing as bad weather, just inappropriate clothing."

"Jeez, you really got me now! In that case, grab your rain gear."

A few minutes later, Evey and Archer were on their bikes pedaling toward Apple Bay. Evey updated Archer on her grandma's notes along the way. They crossed the bridge over the north end of the lake. Even in the rain, Evey counted five people fishing along the sides of the bridge. A mile later, they turned onto Apple Bay Road. From there, Archer led Evey down a side street by the town hardware store. The museum sat across the street.

From the outside, Evey thought the Door County Historical Museum looked like an old colonial house. It was two stories tall and covered in white, wood siding. Green shudders framed every window. Decorative, green trim outlined the front door.

Evey and Archer dropped their bikes in the parking lot and ran to the door, dodging puddles along the way. Evey turned the knob and pushed the heavy, green door open. They entered the foyer, where paintings of various boats and lighthouses hung on the walls. Evey noticed a staircase in the back of the room, and doorways on each side that led to additional rooms.

After circling the foyer, they stopped at a map by the stairs. The map showed the museum's exhibits, including ones on Door County wildlife, apple and cherry orchards, Native American history, and nautical history. It also included a mockup of a nineteenth century town street, several old fire trucks, and a wall filled with old photographs.

Evey pointed to a spot on the map. "Let's . . . start in . . . the . . . nautical room," she said.

Archer nodded, and the two entered a large room to the right of the foyer. The same creaky, wood floors continued into the room. The walls featured blue and white striped wallpaper. A mannequin at the end of the room caught Evey's attention. The figure wore tall black boots, a hat, and a dark blue coat with gold trim and buttons. It reminded Evey of the shadowy man from her vision.

"Look at this stuff," Archer said, pointing to a glass case in the middle of the room. Evey peered inside to study the artifacts. She recognized some old compasses and a variety of maps showing the waters around Door County.

"Not very accurate, back then," Evey mumbled while looking at a map of the entire peninsula.

"What's that?" Archer asked from across the case.

"Just a . . . weird-looking map."

Archer walked over to Evey. "What's wrong with it?" he asked.

"The label says it's an old map of Door County, but the bays and . . . shorelines look off. Particularly, Apple Bay."

Archer shrugged. "I guess. I don't really know."

"Haven't you ever . . . seen a map of Door County?"

"Um, yes—maybe—should I have?" Archer winced as Evey sighed. "Okay, give me the basics," he said. "Door County geography 101."

Am I the only kid who ever looks at maps? Evey thought. She turned her attention back to the case and pointed to the bottom of the map. "Door County is a tall peninsula," she said. "Sturgeon Bay is the big town at the . . . south end."

Archer leaned closer to the map. "My mom calls Sturgeon Bay 'the big city' because they have a Target there."

Evey raised her eyebrow.

"She has a point," Archer continued. "There's nothing up here. No fast-food chains or big box stores. It's just endless arts and craft studios. Seriously, there's probably three of them for every person up here."

Evey smiled. *Some of us like things to be quiet,* she thought. She turned back to the map. "The west side of Door County . . . borders Green Bay."

"Nothing good about that place," Archer said as he adjusted his Chicago Bears hat.

Evey rolled her eyes. "I mean Green Bay the body of . . . water, not the city."

"Oh, sorry. The Packers drive me crazy."

"That's because they're better," Evey mumbled.

"What did you—"

Evey cut in before Archer could finish. "The west side of Door County is . . . where Pancake Harbor and Rainbow Bay are. The east side touches Lake . . . Michigan. That's . . . where we are, by Apple Bay and Turtle Lake."

Archer scrunched his face as he examined the map. "It always annoyed me how they give towns and bodies of water the same name. Green Bay, Apple Bay—are we talking about the towns or the actual bays—who knows! Couldn't they have called the towns Greentown and Appletown? They didn't name Chicago after Lake Michigan—although the Lake Michigan Bears does sound kind of cool."

Evey rolled her eyes. She pointed to a body of water on the map. "This old map shows some kind of . . . harbor connected to Lake Michigan," she said, "but this is where Turtle Lake should be. And there . . . should be half a mile of land between it and Lake Michigan."

"Are you sure it's not three quarters of a mile?" Archer said with a smirk.

Evey slowly turned to Archer. "I'm . . . sure," she said sternly.

"Maybe it's like those old-world maps where everything looks goofy. Like in your history book at school. When those explorers had to guess to finish their maps."

Evey shrugged.

"How do you know so much about maps, anyway?" Archer asked.

"Uh . . ." Evey mumbled. "I . . . like to know—"

"Can I help you two?" said a voice from the foyer.

Evey and Archer jumped and turned around. A woman stood in the entrance to the room. Evey thought that the woman stood very straight and proper. She had a hard time determining the woman's age. Her hair was completely gray and in a tight bun, but her youthful face, numerous ear piercings, and bright yellow sweater made her look much younger.

"Oh," Archer said, "we're just trying to find information on a crystal."

The woman smiled. "Sorry for not introducing myself. My name is Professor Paulsen. Well, you can call me Ann. I just finished giving final exams to my students, so I'm still in school mode. And you two are?"

"Hi, Professor Paulsen—I mean, Ann," Archer said. "Sorry, that feels weird—calling adults by their first name. My parents always tell me not to. Although, I call my cousins by their first names, and one is like thirty. So, he's an—"

"Archer," Evey whispered as she elbowed him.

"Sorry, I'm rambling again. Anyway, I'm Archer and this is Evey."

"That's okay," Professor Paulsen said. "In that case, Mr. Archer and Ms. Evey, tell me about this crystal you mentioned."

Archer nudged Evey. "Show it to her," he said. "She's a professor."

Evey took the crystal necklace off and held it out for Professor Paulsen to see.

"That is quite a beautiful piece," Professor Paulsen said. "May I take a look?" Evey handed the crystal to her. Professor Paulsen reached into her pocket and took out a pair of thick, round-framed glasses and put them on. She inspected the crystal. "I must say, this looks very familiar."

Evey remembered her grandma's note about visiting the museum. "My grandma brought it . . . here, before . . . she died," Evey said. "It was a . . . long time ago."

Professor Paulsen snapped her fingers. "Was she a red-haired lady of about my height?"

"You remember her?" Evey asked.

"I most certainly do. It's not every day somebody shows you something like this. Come to think of it, you look remarkably like her."

Evey felt her face blush. Her Triforce burned. *Except Grandma didn't have these annoying moles,* she thought.

"What was it that she asked about?" Professor Paulsen said.

"The Pirate," Archer said with as deep a voice he could muster.

"That's it," Professor Paulsen said. "The legendary Door County Pirate. She suspected this crystal could've been related to him."

"We were . . . hoping to . . . find more information," Evey said. "My grandma's notes . . . mentioned . . . a letter—from the Pirate."

Professor Paulsen smiled. "Why of course. The letter is one of our prized artifacts. Would you like to read it?"

Evey shook her head yes.

CHAPTER 10

Professor Paulsen led Evey and Archer to the far end of the nautical room, where the Pirate's letter sat in a special display case. "Here it is," she said. "This letter is the only known artifact from the Door County Pirate."

"I still can't believe there was a pirate in Wisconsin," Archer said. "Did he have a cool name, like Blackbeard?"

"Nobody knew his actual name," Professor Paulsen said. "In fact, we know very little about him."

"Then how do we know it was a 'he?'" Archer asked. Evey and Professor Paulsen both looked at him. "What?" he said. "I'm the guy here—shouldn't you two be asking that question?"

"A valid point," Professor Paulsen said. "Most pirates were men, but there are a few examples of prominent women."

"He . . . sounded like a man in . . . my dream," Evey whispered.

Archer shrugged. "You're probably right. It's just a habit to refer to all people and animals as 'her' until proven otherwise. I grew up in a house with a lot of women's power talk."

Do I always use 'he' to refer to animals? Evey thought.

"I've got a good name!" Archer said. "How about Cheesebeard? You know, because Wisconsin and cheese."

Evey smirked. *That one actually is funny,* she thought. She turned to Professor Paulsen. "What is known about . . . the Pirate?"

"The story dates back to the 1850s," Professor Paulsen said. "Migration to Door County picked up during that period. Sailors traveling to and from Green Bay started complaining about a pirate harassing them. Later, a rumor spread about someone seeing precious crystals traded around. The theory was that the Pirate stole goods from merchant ships and traded them with local Native Americans for the crystals. People believed that he acquired quite a treasure. So, the local settlers put together several expeditions to hunt him down, but the Pirate managed to escape them all. Eventually, the U.S. Navy had to chase him."

"And?" Archer asked impatiently. "Did they get him—Cheesebeard?"

"And then comes the letter." Professor Paulsen took a key out of her pocket and unlocked the display case. She carefully removed the worn, yellowed paper and set it on a table. "It was written to a woman named Evelyn—is that what your name stands for, Ms. Evey?"

Evey nodded.

"Whoa! What a coincidence!" Archer said. "It's kind of creepy, actually. I told you that crystal is haunted."

Evey rolled her eyes.

"How did the museum get this?" Archer asked.

"The Navy intercepted the letter before it was delivered," Professor Paulsen said. "They gave it to the museum when it opened in 1930."

Evey and Archer read the letter quietly:

August 14th, 1858

Evelyn,

Time is of the essence. The Navy is closing in on me and I must try to escape with the treasure. This Lieutenant Carlisle has proven a worthy adversary. I have not been able to evade him like the others. All will be lost if he catches me. If I cannot escape, I will see to it that nobody finds the treasure, or me, whatever the cost. I hope you can understand. If our paths do not cross again, just remember to look beneath the sunrise.

O~G

Archer leaned back from the case and turned to Professor Paulsen. "Why's the letter signed 'O~G?'" he asked. "I'm assuming it doesn't stand for Olive Garden."

"Were you expecting Cheesebeard?" Professor Paulsen said.

Evey laughed, then looked back at the letter. She reread it while Archer and Professor Paulsen continued talking.

"No one is sure," Professor Paulsen said. "Presumably, the Pirate knew the letter could be intercepted, so he probably did not want to use his real name. Perhaps it is his initials or some type of code."

"What happened after they intercepted the letter?" Archer asked.

"The story goes that Lieutenant Carlisle ambushed the Pirate when he tried to make his escape. He chased him around the peninsula until the Pirate's ship sunk near Death's Door. Most believe his treasure sunk with him."

"And nobody's ever found his ship?"

"I remember a news story many years ago that somebody thought they found it. They didn't find the treasure, though. And besides, there are so many wrecks around Door County, it's hard to be sure if it really was his."

"So, that means," Archer said, "the treasure is still out there, waiting to be found!"

"In theory," Professor Paulsen said with a shrug. "I for one never believed there was a treasure. Historically speaking, pirates usually spent their money instead of hiding it. But . . ." Professor Paulsen motioned to Evey, ". . . that crystal could prove otherwise."

Evey ignored their conversation as she was fixated on the last sentence in the letter. *Look beneath the sunrise,* she thought. *Just like my vision. That can't be a coincidence. I hope it is—I think—I still don't know whether to be scared or excited. If 'sunrise' refers to a lighthouse, how does it relate to this letter? Is it a secret message? And who is Evelyn? Probably the Pirate's friend or partner, right? Ugh! My head feels like it's going to—*

"You're being quiet," Archer said as he waved his hand in front of Evey's face.

"Uh . . . sorry," she replied. "I was just read . . . rereading this part."

"Which part?" Professor Paulsen asked.

"The last sentence—about . . . sunrise. What do you . . . think it . . . means?"

Professor Paulsen adjusted her glasses and read the end of the letter. "I never thought much of that line," she said. "Perhaps it's just a phrase that has special meaning between these two. Why do you ask?"

"It's hard to . . . it's just . . ." Evey rubbed her temples. "I had a dream. I was on an . . . island. And there was this . . . shadow—no, a . . . a man. It doesn't make . . . sense . . ." Evey's voice trailed off.

"Wait!" Archer yelled.

Evey and Professor Paulsen both jumped.

"Sorry," Archer said. "I got too excited. I do that. Anyway, I forgot about the sunrise part in your vision, Evey. It does makes sense. Tell Professor Paulsen."

"Okay," Evey said. She took a deep breath. "In my dream . . . vision, this man . . . talked about my grandma's crystal. He mentioned a . . . secret. He said to look . . . beneath . . . the sunrise. My grandma . . . wrote about the same . . . vision, years ago."

"Isn't that freaky?" Archer said to Professor Paulsen. "I told Evey the crystal is going to bring some zombies to life."

Professor Paulsen laughed. "I don't know about zombies, but this vision or dream certainly is fascinating. The real question is what could 'sunrise' mean, if it is in fact a code of some sort. Do you have any guesses, Evey?"

"I think a . . . light . . . house," she said.

"What makes you say that?"

Evey explained the moving light in her vision.

"Perhaps you're on to something," Professor Paulsen said. "The general assumption is that the Pirate's treasure sunk

72

with his ship. But I suppose he could have hidden it elsewhere. Maybe he wanted this Evelyn lady to find it."

Archer started jumping. "Wait a minute! So, the letter could actually be a secret message! That's so cool! I saw a movie like this one time. It was about these spies who dropped coded letters under a bridge. They used a bunch of secret cyphers to read them. But then one of them—"

"Archer," Evey said as she nudged him.

"Sorry! This is too exciting. If the Pirate did hide the treasure in a lighthouse, maybe we can still find it!"

Evey shook her head.

"What's wrong?" Archer asked.

"I don't . . . think it's in the . . . light . . . house. I think it's a map or . . . something."

"A treasure map?" Archer repeated. "I thought this letter was our map. This is starting to feel like a video game. How many levels are there? Do we need to find a magical sword and shield along the way?"

Evey laughed. "Either way, I . . . see a . . . problem. Door County has tons of light . . . houses."

Professor Paulsen nodded. "And most of them were built after the Pirate's time," she said. "I don't know of any lighthouses from the 1850s that are still around."

The room quieted as Evey and Archer both frowned.

Professor Paulsen broke the silence. "You can't give up on an idea like that just because you hit a little obstacle."

"What do you mean?" Archer asked.

"Research!" Professor Paulsen's voice boomed throughout the room. "It's what history is all about."

"Okay," Archer said. "Where do we start?"

"Let's go to the gift shop. I think we have something that can help."

Evey and Archer followed Professor Paulsen through the foyer to the gift shop. Large windows overlooking the lake ran along the back wall. Shelves and tables with a wide array of t-shirts, coloring books, stuffed animals, and other gifts cluttered the room. Professor Paulsen stopped by a large bookcase. Evey looked over the books. They included titles about Door County's wildlife, lakes, and apple and cherry orchards. She also noticed a history of Door County's shipwrecks and a nature photography book.

Professor Paulsen took two books off the shelf. "Here's what we need," she said as she handed them to Evey. "This one is a general history of Door County. It might have some content about the Pirate. The other one is a history of Door County's lighthouses. It covers the existing ones, but it also goes back to the first European traders who came through the area in the 1500s. They may give you some clues."

Evey took the books. "Tanks, but I don't . . . have enough . . . money—"

"Don't worry, Ms. Evey. You can borrow them. There are plenty of copies here. Just bring them back in good shape when you're done."

Evey nodded.

"Keep one thing in mind when you're researching," Professor Paulsen continued. "While these are good books, they don't know everything. Just because something isn't in there doesn't mean it's not true. That's when primary sources can be more helpful."

Evey raised her eyebrow.

"Did I say something wrong?" Professor Paulsen asked.

"Oh, no," Archer said. "That's just Evey's way of asking a question. I think she means to ask what a primary source is."

"Yea," Evey said as she lowered her eyebrow. "It's . . . easier," she mumbled.

"No problem at all," Professor Paulsen said. "You see, a book like this—much like the history textbooks you read in school—is called a secondary source. It means the author wrote about past events he or she did not observe, often long after they happened. A primary source is different. It's an artifact from the actual event you are studying."

Evey raised her eyebrow again while Archer scratched his neck.

"Let me give you an example," Professor Paulsen continued. "If we are studying lighthouses, this book is a secondary source. It was written a few years ago, and it summarizes a whole bunch of information on the history of various lighthouses. A primary source would be notes written by an architect who actually built one of them. Does that make sense?"

Evey shook her head yes.

"The letter to Evelyn—that's a primary source, right?" Archer asked.

"Exactly!" Professor Paulsen said. "In fact, most of the items in the museum are primary sources. For example, all the artifacts and clothes in the nautical room are real items sailors once used around Door County. Primary sources like these help you decide for yourself what happened, rather than let somebody else tell you the story."

Archer winced. "That sounds like a lot of work. Isn't it easier to just read a book, or better yet, a quick summary online?"

"Yes and no. History books are very useful in helping us study certain subjects. But you have to be careful. The author could leave out important details, or have a bias that affects how they tell the story."

"Why would somebody do that?" Archer asked.

"Sometimes, people do it because they are trying to convince people to support their view. Most of the time, it happens by accident. Take yourself for example, Mr. Archer. I see you are a football fan." Professor Paulsen pointed to his hat. "The Chicago Bears—you're brave wearing that around here."

"Eh, nobody bothers me," Archer said.

"Well, if you were writing a book about the history of football, you might argue that the Bears are a better team." Professor Paulsen paused and smiled. "Even though the Packers have won a lot more championships."

Evey laughed as she shook her head yes. *Can't talk your way out of that one, Archer,* she thought.

"Jeez, you got me there," Archer said, rolling his eyes.

"Does the museum . . . have other primary . . . sources about the Pirate?" Evey asked.

"We don't have anything else here," Professor Paulsen said, "but the library at my university might. I can check in the office."

Evey and Archer followed Professor Paulsen to a small room behind the gift shop. Professor Paulsen took a seat at a computer on a long table running along the wall.

"It will just take a minute," Professor Paulsen said. After flying through a series of web pages and typing in some search questions, she stopped to investigate the results. "Excellent! We do have something."

"What is it?" Archer asked.

"It's Lieutenant Carlisle's military papers. You remember, the man who chased the Pirate. I knew he was from Wisconsin, so I was hoping we might have something on him. His papers are a collection of everything he wrote while in the Navy. Letters and reports to his superiors and such. It should discuss his mission to catch the Pirate."

"That sounds fasten—I mean . . . fascinating." Evey said.

Professor Paulsen swiveled her chair around. "History is fascinating! I certainly agree with you on that, Ms. Evey."

Archer scratched his neck. "I guess," he said. "But they don't exactly teach it like this at my school. It's more boring facts than cool pirate mysteries."

"I'm sorry to hear that," Professor Paulsen said. "History definitely can become bogged down by facts when not taught properly. The goal of history is to help us make sense of our world and the people in it. To explain things like where that crystal came from. Learning about mysteries like that is when history is at its best."

"Professor," Evey said, "how do we get . . . Carl . . . Carlisle's papers?"

"I will have my university mail it here. It should arrive within a week. Give us a call in a few days to check."

Evey nodded.

"In the meantime," Professor Paulsen continued, "see what you can find in those books. I will print a copy of the letter to Evelyn before you leave, as well. That should keep you busy, for now."

Once Professor Paulsen printed the copy of the letter, Evey and Archer thanked her, then headed for their bikes in the parking lot. "Can you believe it?" Archer asked. "You might be walking around with pirate treasure! And we might be able to find more!"

Evey smiled at Archer, but a small worry nagged at her. *I think the treasure is something bigger than money*, she thought. *Still, it would be awesome to find it—that is if I can handle this. It is kind of scary. And all of this research sounds overwhelming. Ugh! Stop thinking that way! I just need—*

"Evey? Can you hear me?" Archer asked.

"What?" she replied.

"I said, since I'm going home tomorrow, I can research the Pirate on the internet. My house is in the twenty-first century, unlike up here."

Evey laughed as she thought about Grandpa's refusal to pay for internet. *The signal is no good by the lake,* she thought, replaying his defense.

"Anyway, what do you think?" Archer asked.

Evey nodded. "I'll see what I can . . . find in . . . these books."

"What else are you going to do while you're up here?"

Evey looked at the lake behind the museum. While the rain had stopped, the gusty wind still pushed large waves into the bay. She turned back to Archer. "Learn to . . . sail," she said. "I think we might . . . need that."

CHAPTER 11

After a night of research and mini-golf with Grandpa, Evey woke up early Monday morning for her first sailing lesson. As Grandpa drove her to the Apple Bay Marina, she stared out the window, nervously biting her lip.

All the time I thought about us having a sailboat, I never actually thought about sailing it myself, Evey thought. Her stomach churned.

The marina sat across from the town park, not far from the museum. Grandpa pulled his truck into the parking lot and found a spot. Evey hopped out to look around. A long wall of boulders protected the marina from the lake. Dozens of boats rested along its two main piers.

"How big is the boat I'm . . . sailing?" Evey asked Grandpa.

"It's supposed to be a catamaran similar to ours. Why don't you go upstairs for a bird's eye view while I check in at the office?" Grandpa pointed to the observation lookout on top of the marina office.

Evey nodded and walked up the stairs to the lookout. From there, she saw all of the docked boats, as well as several in the bay. While enjoying the view, a sign attached to the railing caught her attention. It was a wood plaque about the size of a computer screen. Evey walked closer to read it:

Apple Bay Marina, est. 1850
Door County's Oldest Marina

I didn't know this was the oldest marina, Evey thought. *File that fact in the useless trivia part of my brain.*

The groan of an engine brought Evey's attention back to the boats. Below her, a large, blue truck backed a trailer toward the water to unload a small fishing boat. Evey watched until the trailer hit the water line. Her eyes then wandered around the marina looking for sailboats. Past the boat ramp, she saw a large dock with two small speedboats, four wave runners, and six sailboats. Two of the sailboats were catamarans.

Evey jogged down from the lookout and over to the dock for a closer look. The catamarans seemed similar to Grandpa's, but a few feet longer. Plus, they had benches on top of each hull.

"You found them!" Grandpa said from behind Evey. She turned to see him walking along the dock with a young woman. She was wearing a blue jacket with the marina's anchor logo.

"Hi! You must be Evey," the woman said. "I'm Hannah. I'll be your instructor for the next three weeks."

Evey smiled and shook Hannah's hand.

"What do you think of the boat?" Hannah asked.

Evey bit her lip. "Uh . . . it's big," she said.

"Only a little bigger than ours," Grandpa said. "Nothing to be nervous about."

"Your grandpa's right," Hannah said. "The sixteen-footer looks big, but people get the hang of it in no time."

"So, what's the plan?" Grandpa asked Hannah.

"First, we need to get you two into some life vests," Hannah said. "Then, we'll get in the boat to review the basics. And then we can take a quick cruise around the harbor. We'll share sailing duties today. But throughout the next three weeks, Evey will take over more of the work, and we'll go further into the open water to make sure she can handle the stronger winds and waves."

Evey bit her lip again. Meanwhile, Hannah directed them to a large rack of life vests on the dock.

While searching for the right size, Evey leaned over to Grandpa. "Did you know . . . this marina is the . . . oldest in Door County?" she asked.

"Really?" Grandpa said. "I've never heard that. I would've thought it would be Sturgeon Bay."

Evey turned to Hannah. "Did you know that?" she asked.

"I did, actually. 1850 was the year. I remember because they had a huge party in 2000 for the 150th anniversary. My parents used to talk about it."

After finding life vests, the three boarded the sailboat. Hannah explained that port and starboard refer to the left and right sides of the boat, aft the back, and bow the front. Hannah also reviewed the hull, rudder, mast, boom, jib sail, and the mainsail. Evey bit her lip as she tried to keep up.

"Don't worry," Hannah said. "In a few weeks, you'll have it all down. Trust me!"

Evey shrugged.

Hannah started prepping the boat to leave the dock. "Evey, do you have any experience on sailboats?" she asked.

"My family . . . went on a big . . . sailboat once," Evey replied. "I don't remember . . . how things . . . work."

"What makes you want to learn?"

"Grandpa's helping me . . . fix an old . . . catamaran. I want to take it in . . . Turtle Lake."

"No kidding! My family lives on Turtle Lake. That's where I learned to sail when I was little."

"Evey, show Hannah the crystal," Grandpa said. "If she's been on the lake a lot, maybe she's seen something like it."

Evey pulled the crystal necklace out from under her shirt and showed it to Hannah. "We think . . . this is part of a treasure."

"Wow," Hannah said as she looked at the crystal. "That's really cool."

"You ever come across anything like that on Turtle Lake?" Grandpa asked.

"No, definitely not," Hannah said. "I've found my share of cool rocks and shells, but no crystals. You think it's part of a treasure?"

Evey nodded. "The Door County . . . Pirate."

"That sounds familiar," Hannah said. "I think I learned about that when I was in grade school. I should introduce you to my little sister and brother. She loves that kind of stuff, and he's into boats too."

Grandpa patted Evey's shoulder. "At this rate you'll have a whole crew to explore with."

Evey smiled.

"How's the work coming along on the boat?" Hannah asked. "Is it old?"

"Around twenty-five years," Grandpa said. "We just started working on it this weekend."

"That's neat that the two of you are doing it together." Hannah turned to Grandpa. "Are you familiar with sailboats?"

"Just a little," Grandpa said. "I was on a sailboat a handful of times when I was younger, but those were monohulled boats. I know things are a little different on catamarans."

"Very true," Hannah replied. "A catamaran obviously has two hulls instead of one. That does make things different."

"How?" Evey asked.

"For starters, catamarans feel more stable," Hannah said. "They don't roll around as much as a monohulled boat."

Grandpa nodded along with Hannah. "It's like the pontoon boat back at the house, Evey. It has two hulls. You know how it barely rocks in the water."

"Exactly," Hannah said. "Also, catamarans tend to be faster. Because less of the boat sits underwater, they have less drag. Look over there, for example." Hannah pointed to a large catamaran further out in the lake. The boat flew through the water like a wave runner. Two sailors hung over the side of the boat, just above the water, lying nearly sideways.

"Whoa," Grandpa said. "What are those things called that they're hanging on? Starts with a T, right?"

"You're thinking of the trapeze wires," Hannah said. "They use a harness and a series of wires so they can hang over the side of the boat. It allows them to push the sails harder without tipping the boat over."

"Do I . . . have to do . . . that?" Evey bit her lip again.

"No, that's pretty advanced stuff," Hannah said. "Although, if the wind is strong, you do sometimes have to

83

balance the boat. If the wind is blowing the boat to the starboard side, sit on the port side to help weigh it down, and vice versa." Hannah moved around the boat to demonstrate.

Evey nodded.

"And there's one last thing," Hannah said. "Our catamaran doesn't have a daggerboard, so it can sail in shallower water than monohulled boats."

Evey raised her eyebrow.

Hannah looked confused. "Are you asking what a daggerboard is?" she said.

"Uh . . . yea," Evey replied as she lowered her eyebrow. *Isn't a raised eyebrow like a universal language for asking a question?* she thought.

"No worries," Hannah continued. "A daggerboard is like a fin on the bottom of the boat. It helps keep a monohulled sailboat steady. Since it sticks into the water, sailors have to be careful not to hit it on rocks or anything down below. But most catamarans can sail right up to a beach. All you have to do is lift the rudder up like this."

Evey watched Hannah flip the two rudder blades upward, then drop them back into the water.

Once Hannah finished showing Evey the other parts of the boat, she raised the sails and took them out of the marina. They cleared the long boulder wall and entered the bay. The boat moved slowly in the calm wind, and only slightly rocked to the side. Evey looked back toward the marina. She could already see most of the town of Apple Bay, including the museum. Chester's, the popular burger and ice cream restaurant caught her eye from its spot up on a hill. Evey could see the patio was already packed, and the line for ice cream trailed out the door of the red and white building.

"Do you see what I see?" Grandpa said, looking in the same direction.

"I see a . . . huge line," Evey said.

"I made a reservation for after the lesson. I figured we'd be hungry."

Evey smiled. *Always prepared when it comes to food,* she thought.

As they continued sailing around the bay, Hannah discussed the nautical terms tacking, upwind, and downwind. Evey promised to study the vocabulary list at Grandpa's. Hannah spent a lot of time explaining the boom—a pole that ran along the bottom of the mainsail and controlled its position. She helped Evey move it back-and-forth to best catch the wind and keep the boat stable. Hannah also showed Evey how to adjust the smaller jib sail.

After thirty minutes of cruising, Hannah turned the boat toward Apple Bay Beach. "Let me show you what I mean about sailing in shallow water," she said.

Evey looked at the beach. She noticed several monohulled boats anchored far from the sand. "Is that as . . . far as . . . they can go?" she asked Hannah.

"Most likely. The water is only a couple of feet deep now. Look over the side. You can see the bottom."

Evey looked down. The sandy bottom looked close enough to touch. "Can we go . . . further?" she asked.

"Just watch," Hannah replied.

Evey looked at the shallow water again. She bit her lip and grabbed the bench as tight as she could. *We're going to run aground!* she thought.

About twenty feet from shore, Hannah pulled the rudders to the upward position so they stuck out of the water. With a little bump and a quiet grinding sound, the boat glided onto the beach.

"Perfect landing!" Hannah said.

Evey hopped out of the boat. She pressed her feet into the sand, then watched a wave of cold water sweep around her ankles.

"That's so cool," Grandpa said as he joined Evey. "This is way better than a regular boat."

Evey nodded and smiled. She imagined all the places in Turtle Lake she could take Grandpa's boat. She saw herself sailing around Coyote Island and parking it on the rocky beach, but then she remembered having to jump off the cliff.

Hannah walked over to Evey. "Do you want to handle the rudder and mainsail on the way back?"

Evey bit her lip. *That sounds terrifying*, she thought.

Grandpa nudged her shoulder. "Well?" he said.

Evey took a deep breath and shook her head yes.

CHAPTER 12

With Hannah's help, Evey controlled the sailboat most of the way back to the marina. After the lesson, she thanked Hannah and walked to Chester's with Grandpa. Evey normally ordered a mushroom burger, but she decided to pick up a menu when she remembered her embarrassing booger order from a few days earlier.

"Not getting your usual?" Grandpa asked.

Evey shrugged as she looked over the menu. *This is ridiculous,* she thought. *What am I—scared of a word?* When the waitress came, Grandpa requested a whitefish sandwich. Evey sighed and put her menu down. "A . . . mushroom . . . buh . . . ur . . . grr," she carefully said.

"Is this the only place you don't order fish?" Grandpa asked after the waitress left.

"I guess," Evey mumbled. The smell of burgers coming from the kitchen reminded her of why the order was worth the effort.

"Food aside, did you like the lesson?"

Evey was busy stuffing lemon wedges in her water. She gave a thumbs up as she took a drink.

"Great," Grandpa said. "I'll go with you tomorrow, but after that you'll be on your own. I have to start my chores.

We have a lot to do before everybody comes back for the Fourth."

Evey nodded, then the two spent the next ten minutes reviewing the sailing lesson and Evey's vocabulary list. "Aren't you glad we have a catamaran?" Grandpa asked when they finished. "That was so cool how we sailed right up to the beach."

Evey smiled as she took another drink of water.

"And believe me, it's nice not having to worry about breaking a daggerboard," Grandpa said.

Evey raised her eyebrow.

"When I was a teenager, I went sailing with some friends up here," Grandpa said. "The guy I was with wasn't paying attention and he took the boat into a shallow, rocky area. He smashed his daggerboard. I thought we hit an iceberg!" Grandpa made a loud crunching noise, shook the table, and fell back into his seat with a look of terror.

Evey laughed and accidentally spit out some of her water. Most made it back into her glass, but some spilled onto the table, causing her and Grandpa to laugh more.

"Then what?" Evey asked after settling down.

"We made it to shore," Grandpa said, "but it was a slow and wobbly ride. Thankfully, the weather was fine. A daggerboard is really important when the wind is strong. I didn't sail again for a while after that. As I recall, that kid got in big trouble. It was his dad's boat. I think he . . ."

Evey's attention drifted from Grandpa to the kitchen once she noticed the distinct smell of her mushroom burger. She looked to the far end of the dining room and saw the waitress walking over with their food.

"Lunch time!" Grandpa said once he saw the waitress.

The waitress set both meals down on the table. Evey grabbed the bottle of ketchup and smothered her burger and fries while Grandpa slathered tartar sauce on his food.

After taking a few hungry bites, Evey asked, "Speaking of boats, where are we . . . with ours?"

Grandpa finished a large piece of his sandwich. "I have all of the parts except the sails. I say we patch and paint the hull. After that, we can put the new trampoline on, then replace the worn ropes in the rigging. That way, it'll be ready for the sails when they arrive."

Evey nodded as she poured another mound of ketchup on her fries.

"How do you even taste the food with that much ketchup?" Grandpa asked. "You are too similar to your dad. He does the same thing."

Evey raised her eyebrow.

"Too similar in more ways than one, I might add," Grandpa said.

The two took a break from talking while they finished their lunch. After polishing off his last bite, Grandpa leaned back into the booth. "Back to the boat," he said. "According to the lady at the store, the sails should show up by the time you finish your lessons."

"Okay," Evey said with a smile. "Meanwhile, can we explore . . . light . . . houses?"

"Lighthouses? What made you interested in those?" Grandpa asked. Evey caught him up on her trip to the museum and the letter to Evelyn. Grandpa rubbed his chin as he listened. "Hmm," he said. "Your grandma certainly had a thing for lighthouses, but that was before she found the crystal. Did you see anything in her notes about it?"

"Kind of."

"What's that mean?"

Evey sat silent for a moment. *Should I tell him more?* she wondered. *If I mention that Grandma and I both heard "sunrise" in our visions, he'll probably think I'm crazy.*

"Evey?" Grandpa said.

"It's ard—I mean . . . hard . . . to explain," she said. "But Professor Paulsen . . . thinks I could be on to . . . something."

Grandpa nodded. "Well, if this professor agrees, it must be a decent lead. I think we can find time to visit some lighthouses."

Evey smiled.

"Do you want to bring your friend, Archer, with?" Grandpa asked.

Evey shook her head no. "He went . . . home for a . . . few weeks."

"Okay," Grandpa said. He rubbed his hands together. "Time for more important things—ice cream!"

Evey massaged her stomach. "I need a break."

Grandpa laughed. "Sailing is a lot of work, so we are treating ourselves."

After a few minutes of rest, Evey headed to the ice cream counter while Grandpa took care of the lunch bill and went to the bathroom. The usual, large group of customers crowded the counter. Evey squeezed through several people to take a number for the wait line. Grandpa asked her to order his usual cup of chocolate cookie dough. Evey, like her dad, was an ice cream traditionalist and stuck to vanilla.

When a server called Evey's number, she weaved through the crowd again to reach the counter, but bumped into another kid. "Tarry . . ." she started to say, but she froze when the boy turned around.

It was Finn—the East Siders' leader. Evey could tell he recognized her as his eyes widened. They stared at each other in awkward silence for several seconds.

"Oh, uh, funny seeing you here," Finn finally said.

Evey felt her face turn red as she stared at him. Her Triforce moles burned. She tried to speak, but her jaw locked up. She ground her teeth instead.

"So, no hard feelings about the island, I hope," Finn said.

No hard feelings! Evey thought. *Are you kidding me? I'll have no hard feelings after I throw a sundae in his face.* Finn turned back to the ice cream counter. *Now he's turning his back on me! Ugh! Say something to him!*

Evey tried hard to relax her jaw. Finally, she managed to move her lips. "Hut up," she mumbled.

"What did you say?" Finn asked as he turned back around.

Evey's jaw hurt. *Hut up—get it together, Evey! Why don't I tell him I'm going wimming again while I'm at it? Talk louder and pronounce the 's' for once in your life!*

"That's what I thought," Finn said. "Just stay away from our island and we'll be good."

Evey ground her teeth until her gums hurt. She started raising a fist.

"Finn, over here!" yelled a voice from behind Evey. She turned to see Hannah making her way over with a young girl. Hannah put her arm on Finn's shoulder. "Fancy seeing you here!" she said when she noticed Evey. "Do you know my brother?"

91

Finn answered before Evey could think of anything to say. "Yea, we ran into each other on Turtle Lake," he said.

Evey stood frozen. *Hannah—Finn—siblings. I can't even start to process what just happened here.*

Finn winked at Evey. "She's quite the kayaker," he said.

Did he just wink at me? Evey thought as she tried to hide her anger. *Who is this kid?* She raised her eyebrow as Finn smiled at her.

Hannah turned back to Evey. "What a coincidence! Oh, by the way, this is my little sister I told you about—Grace."

Evey thought Grace was about ten years old. She had the same brown hair as Hannah and Finn.

"Grace," Hannah said, "Evey is the girl I was just telling you about. She's got a lead on some old artifacts around Turtle Lake. Maybe even some treasure."

Evey noticed Finn turn and pay more attention to the conversation.

"That sounds awesome!" Grace said. "Maybe I could go with one day! I love old stuff like that."

"Uh . . ." Evey struggled to respond.

"Finn, maybe you can work it out," Hannah said. "Evey's fixing up an old catamaran with her grandpa. You and Grace can show her around the lake."

"Learning to sail—interesting," Finn said with a smirk. "Hannah, I'm getting really hungry. Can we go? I'm sure I can catch up with Evey on the lake."

"Okay, okay," Hannah said. "I'll see you tomorrow, Evey."

Evey managed a small wave as the three walked out of the room. She stood motionless next to the counter, trying hard to hold back tears.

What just happened? Evey thought. *And why didn't I say something to him! Why do I have to freeze! Why can't I just talk normal like—*

"Evey," Grandpa said from behind her. "Was that Hannah? Do you know those kids she was with?"

Evey stood silently, shaking her fists.

Grandpa put his arm on her shoulder. "You okay?" he asked.

Evey pushed his arm off and ran out of the restaurant. She felt tears trickling down her cheeks as she walked through the parking lot and across the street. She found a park bench near the water and sat down with her head in her hands.

A few minutes later, Grandpa walked over with a cup of chocolate cookie dough and another of vanilla. He took a seat on the bench and handed Evey the vanilla. "There's no reason to skip ice cream," he said. "You want to go for a walk while we eat?"

Evey nodded. The two stood up and started a slow stroll. Evey kept her face down and played with her ice cream. They walked in silence for several minutes before Grandpa cleared his throat. "Do you want to talk about what happened?" he asked.

Evey shook her head no.

"I know, you don't like to talk when you're upset," Grandpa said. "Your dad is like that too. Always was. The more I think about it, you two are a lot alike."

Evey ground her teeth. *Stop talking about me being like my dad*, she thought.

"He always said that he didn't like to talk about it until he could process it, or something like—"

"I'm mot lite my ad!" Evey blurted out. She sighed and rubbed her temples. "I mean . . . you know," she mumbled. *My dad would just be disappointed in me right now*, she thought.

"Sorry," Grandpa said. "Different subject, then." He pointed to a bench and the two took a seat.

Evey kept her head down as she nibbled at her ice cream.

Grandpa opened his mouth several times to begin talking, but stopped himself. Finally, he said, "Remember, it's okay to feel angry, sad, or whatever. Sometimes people try too hard to calm down, think positive, or stop worrying. That's not always possible."

Evey's eyes filled with tears again. She turned her head toward the water to look away from Grandpa. They both sat quietly for the next few minutes.

Once Evey's tears stopped, Grandpa moved closer. "Troubles aside, I would say this was still a successful morning," he said. "Why don't we head to the house and take Howie for a walk?"

Evey nodded.

"And after that," Grandpa continued, "we should pick a mini-golf course to play tonight. We need to keep practicing if I'm going to take the turtle hat back from your uncle."

"Again?" Evey mumbled.

"We need it. I can't stand the thought of your uncle bragging about a three-peat."

Evey chuckled.

"See, that's better," Grandpa said. "Let's go home."

CHAPTER 13

Evey picked up the copy of Lieutenant Carlisle's papers from the museum a few days later. Over the next two weeks, she settled in to a routine at Grandpa's. In the morning, she researched the crystal and the Pirate, then went to her sailing lesson. After lunch, she worked on the sailboat with Grandpa. In the evening, they practiced for the Championship. Grandpa took her to several lighthouses too, but Evey did not find any clues.

By the third and final week of Evey's lessons, she and Grandpa had nearly finished the sailboat. They patched the dents on the hull, replaced the trampoline and the rigging, and gave the boat a fresh coast of white paint. Grandpa also helped Evey paint red streaks across the hulls to make the boat, in his words, "more feisty."

Evey did not make as much progress with her research, and she began to doubt whether she could solve the mystery of her grandma's crystal. She anxiously waited for Archer to return to see if he found anything helpful while at home.

Thursday afternoon, Evey and Grandpa started applying sealant to the boat's hulls, the last step before the sails arrived. With Archer set to return the next day, Evey tried to forget about her research so she could focus on finishing the boat. She slowly moved her brush back-and-forth like Grandpa showed her. However, after a few minutes, splattered sealant already covered her hands and shirt.

At least the hull looks shiny, Evey thought as she tried to scrape the sticky sealant off her hands.

"Surprise!"

Evey jumped and dropped her brush. She turned around and saw Archer standing in the garage with his hands in the air. She bent over to pick up her brush and noticed the sealant now covered her pants. She stood up and crossed her arms.

"Lighten up. That was funny!" Archer said.

"I thought you . . . were coming . . . tomorrow," Evey said.

"I convinced my parents to come a day early. Actually, I don't know if I convinced them so much as I just bothered them. I've been telling them about the stuff I found. I think they're tired of me!"

Evey laughed.

Archer turned to the boat. "This looks amazing. You've been busy, Evey."

"Excuse me," Grandpa said.

"Oh, I'm sorry," Archer said. "It looks like you've both been busy."

"That's more like it," Grandpa said as he continued sealing the starboard hull.

Archer turned back to Evey. "Tell me everything. How are your sailing lessons going? Did you find anything in your grandma's notes or the lighthouse book? Did you get Carlisle's papers? Did you visit the lighthouses? Did you—"

"Slow down," Evey said as she waved her hands. "I don't . . . think that . . . fast."

"Sorry, I'm just excited. I found some interesting stuff researching at home. Because, you know, at home we actually have internet. Internet is like a museum and library mixed together, and way easier. Jeez, I miss the internet when—"

Evey rolled her eyes.

"I'm rambling again! Sorry," Archer said.

"You could've called me," Evey said. "I gave you my grandpa's . . . phone number."

Archer gently slapped his forehead. "Yea, duh. I guess I forget about phones with the reception being so spotty here. Your grandpa must be the only person in the world with a landline nowadays. Anyway, stop distracting me!"

"Let it out!" Evey said.

"Okay. So, at first all I could find was the same story Professor Paulsen told us about the Pirate robbing ships and sinking with his treasure."

Evey nodded. "The . . . museum book . . . said the . . . same."

"But, after digging more," Archer continued, "I found a weird theory from a website all about unexplained history. It sounded silly, so I had my mom look at it. She said the website's authors were legitimate historians, and that they cited their sources correctly, so she approved. However, she also pointed out a big disclaimer on the website that said none of the theories had much evidence, so that was kind of a buzzkill. But whatever, it agreed that the Pirate didn't actually have any treasure on his boat when it sank."

"Did they mention . . . sunrise?"

"Nothing about sunrise, but the website did say the Pirate never actually stole anything. It said he chased a lot of ships, but there were no records of him actually catching anybody. I thought that was weird."

Evey nodded. *That is weird—and very familiar sounding,* she thought.

"The website's theory is that the Pirate . . ." Archer paused. Evey motioned for him to keep going. "I was pausing for dramatic effect," he said. "This is big stuff."

Evey rolled her eyes.

"The theory," Archer continued, "is that the Pirate didn't actually want to steal anything. All he really wanted to do was scare people away because he was protecting something." Archer pointed to the crystal dangling from Evey's neck. "I thought that matched perfectly with your vision about the Pirate protecting a secret—hopefully, a secret involving more expensive crystals!"

Evey looked down at her grandma's crystal. "Uh . . ." she mumbled as she processed Archer's story.

"If I had a microphone, I would drop it right now," he said. "I think I crushed my research."

Grandpa laughed in the background, but Evey kept her eyes fixed on the crystal.

Archer twirled his thumbs. "Well?" he said.

"I'm tinking—no . . . thinking," Evey said. "That . . . sounds . . . familiar."

"I still say that thing is going to bring back the dead. But anyway, what do we believe—the standard history books that say the Pirate's treasure sank with his boat, or the odd but legitimate looking website that lines up with your visions?"

"Remember . . . Professor Paulsen's advice," Evey said. "It's best to use primary . . . sources."

"You're the one with Carlisle's papers. Did they help?"

"Your story . . . sounds . . . familiar. I think it was . . . Ugh! I can't remember. Wait here." Evey ran out of the garage and into the house. She came back with the copy of Carlisle's papers. "Read . . . this entry from . . . Carlisle," she said as she handed the book to Archer.

Archer leaned forward and read aloud:

> Something is rather odd about my mission to track down this pirate. My men and I have spoken with sailors from several merchant ships, as well as numerous people working in the area's ports. Not one person among them can actually name a ship the pirate has overtaken. I protested. Surely a pirate who causes such agitation as to force the Navy to action must have ransacked a great many ships. Nevertheless, these gentlemen described being chased by the pirate, but never actually overtaken. At first, I marveled at how terrible this pirate is at his work. However, upon reflection, I am beginning to wonder if stealing is not this pirate's goal. There may be more to this case than meets the eye.

Archer turned to Evey once he finished reading the entry. "In your vision," he said, "didn't the shadowy man—I feel like at this point we can call him the Pirate. I think your magical crystal is letting you talk with dead people. Bringing them back to life must be step two."

Evey rolled her eyes again.

"Anyway," Archer said, "didn't the Pirate say you had to bring the crystal to the secret place?"

Evey nodded.

"Then, Carlisle's papers support the website's theory. The secret is this special place—a place probably full of magical, haunted crystals. That must have been what he was protecting!"

Evey nodded again. "To find it, we need . . . what's under the light . . . house."

"We have to find it," Archer said, his voice growing more excited. "The world could depend on it!"

Evey raised both of her eyebrows.

"Okay, maybe not the whole world," Archer said. "But it still sounds important. And it might make us rich—assuming we don't die—so that's pretty cool. Any leads from your research to help us find the lighthouse?"

"I did . . . find . . . something. Let's go over . . . here." Evey put her notes and books on Grandpa's workbench. She and Archer sat on some stools to look over everything. "My grandpa and I . . . saw some . . . lighthouses, but didn't . . . find clues."

Archer sighed. "Okay, not a promising start."

"But," Evey said as she flipped through the lighthouse book. "This covers dozens of light . . . houses—what they do, how . . . they're built, and hi—I mean . . ." Evey rubbed her jaw.

Archer looked at the book while Evey paused. "Does it say anything about older lighthouses from the Pirate's time?" he asked.

Evey nodded. "It mentioned that early . . . settlers built the first . . . light . . . houses to help loggers. But like Professor Paulsen . . . said, they're gone."

"Still not promising, but continue."

"Carlisle . . . mentioned loggers. I went back to . . . his papers. I came across something about loggers and . . . Coyote Bay."

"What's Coyote Bay?" Archer asked. "Do you mean Turtle Lake?"

Evey shook her head no. "Read this," she said.

Archer took the book and read aloud:

> Today we stopped a lumber ship on Lake Michigan to learn more about the pirate. I spoke with the captain of the vessel. He told me locals refer to the pirate as the "Coyote Pirate" because he is often seen near Coyote Bay. He said that loggers once worked out of Coyote Bay, but have avoided the area for the last few years due to this pirate. I must continue my investigation to learn more. Then, I shall explore this Coyote Bay directly to see if I can find him.

"Interesting," Archer said. "I think I see where you're going with this. No, actually I don't get it at all."

Evey pointed to the book. "The Pirate . . . was in . . . Coyote Bay, which loggers . . . used. And the . . . first . . . lighthouses . . . were built for logging. So—"

"There was probably a lighthouse in Coyote Bay!" Archer shouted. "Sorry to cut you off. I just got it. You're a genius, Evey!" Archer paused. "Although—"

"Where's Coyote Bay?" Evey cut in. She shrugged. "My grandpa's been coming . . . here for . . . sixty years. He says it doesn't . . . exist."

Archer scratched his neck. "And we're back to not very promising."

"Who . . . wrote the . . . website article you read?" Evey asked. "Can he . . . help?"

"Who said it's a he?" Archer replied.

"Uh . . ." Evey mumbled.

"Sorry, it actually was a guy. I can't help myself, sometimes."

Evey rubbed her temples.

"Anyway, it was some guy named Dr. Hart," Archer continued, "which is a great name for a doctor—except he's not a medical doctor, but like a history doctor. Why do they even call them doctors? Do they make sure textbooks are healthy and—"

"Archer," Evey cut in, "can we . . . contact him?"

"I thought about that," Archer said, "so my mom helped me look him up. He sounded really important and smart, but he's dead now."

Evey pressed her hands on the table. *There goes that lead,* she thought.

Archer shrugged. "He was pretty old. He actually wrote the article years ago. Any other ideas?"

Evey nodded. "I have a . . . theory, but it doesn't . . . make sense."

"That's fine, because none of this makes sense," Archer said as he rubbed his eyes.

"The island in Turtle Lake that . . . the East Siders . . . threw me off—do you . . . know its name?"

Archer twirled his thumbs. "I'm trying to think of something clever and funny, but I've got nothing."

"Coyote Island," Evey said.

"Really? Where did you learn that?"

"Coyote Grill. I don't . . . think it's . . . official. It's not on any maps. But, at Coyote Grill there's a . . . a poster about an old legend. It says coyotes . . . haunt the island."

"At the rate we're going, it's probably more than a legend. Although, if there are ghost coyotes, why don't they chase away the East Siders?"

Evey shook Archer's shoulder. "Stay with me," she said.

"Right," Archer said. "Research, pirates, history doctors—where were we?"

"Coyote Bay," Evey said through a chuckle.

Archer nodded. "Yes, Coyote Bay. Cool, but that still makes no sense. Turtle Lake can't be Coyote Bay. I'm no map wizard like you, but last I checked lakes and bays are different."

"I know, but . . . there has to be a . . . connection."

"Did Carlisle make a mistake? Maybe he meant to say Turtle Lake."

Evey shook her head no. "In another entry, he said he . . . sailed into Coyote Bay."

"Oh," Archer said. "Yea, last I checked, nobody can sail across the ground from Lake Michigan to Turtle Lake. Unless you have one of those cool boats that are also cars. That would be awesome. But where is Coyote Bay, then?"

"I looked at every map of Door County I could . . . find. Coyote Bay is not on any of them."

"Hmm," Archer said as he twirled his thumbs again. "And you know maps, so if you can't find it—wait!" Archer jumped to his feet. "It is on a map!"

Evey raised her eyebrow.

"I'm serious, Evey. The map at the museum, remember? The old-timey one that looked all weird. You pointed it out to me."

Evey dropped her eyebrow as she tried to remember the map. She envisioned looking at it in the display case. She remembered telling Archer the area by Turtle Lake looked like a bay. "You're right!" she yelled as she jumped up from her stool. "I can't believe I . . . forgot that."

"That's okay. It sounds like you have too much research in your head. But your love of maps must be rubbing off on me."

Evey forced a smile. *Seriously, how did I forget something map-related?* she thought. *Maps may be a weird thing, but it's my thing.*

"Anyway," Archer said, "if that old-timey map is right, then maybe Turtle Lake used to be Coyote Bay. Is that even possible?"

"It's possible," Grandpa said from behind the sailboat. Evey and Archer both turned toward him. "Lake Michigan's water level has changed a lot over the years," Grandpa continued. "A few feet higher and it floods some of the shoreline. A few feet lower and areas that were covered in water become dry."

"Oh," Evey said. "I guess . . . that explains it. It seems too . . . simple."

Grandpa shrugged and went back to sealing the boat hull.

"Let me try to get everything straight," Archer said. "The Pirate—or Coyote Pirate—operated out of Coyote Bay, which apparently is Turtle Lake. He never actually captured any ships or stole anything, because he was just trying to scare them away to protect his special place filled with haunted crystals."

Evey nodded.

"And if the Coyote Pirate operated out of Coyote Bay," Archer continued, "he might have used the local lighthouse as his secret hideout."

Evey nodded again.

"Now we just have to figure out where this lighthouse is, and if anything is left of it. I think I know the place to start."

Evey checked her watch. "The museum closes . . . soon. We can't . . . make it if we bike." She looked toward Grandpa with a big smile. "Uh—" she started to say.

"Can't you go tomorrow?" Grandpa asked.

Evey frowned. "I'm . . . sailing in the . . . morning, and you . . . wanted to practice ping-pong after."

Grandpa sighed and put his brush down. "Would you like me to drive you to the museum?"

"Yes please!" Evey and Archer shouted.

CHAPTER 14

Grandpa pulled his truck into the museum parking lot with only five minutes to spare. Evey and Archer hopped out and snatched their bikes from the back, then ran to the museum door. Evey pushed the heavy door open and walked in.

"Professor Paulsen," Evey said.

After a few moments of silence, Archer yelled, "Professor Paulsen!"

Professor Paulsen appeared at the top of the stairs. "Oh, Ms. Evey and Mr. Archer—you startled me! What can I help—"

"Coyote Bay!" Archer yelled before Professor Paulsen could finish. "Sorry, I'm a little wound up."

Professor Paulsen walked down the stairs with a confused look on her face. "What's Coyote Bay?" she asked when she reached the first floor.

Evey updated Professor Paulsen on their research. The professor sat down on a nearby chair and listened closely. "Interesting theory," she said. "But unfortunately, I don't know what Coyote Bay refers to."

Evey and Archer both dropped their jaws. "You don't know!" Archer said.

Professor Paulsen popped up from her chair and stood straighter than normal. "Being a history professor does not mean that I know everything," she said. "Besides, my specialty is European history. This is my summer job."

"Sorry," Archer said.

Evey pointed to the nautical room. "We just need to . . . see the old map."

"Oh, certainly," Professor Paulsen replied. "Right this way. I must say, you've learned well. When the history books don't give you the answers you need, you have to go straight to the primary sources."

Professor Paulsen led them into the nautical room, then took a set of keys from her pocket and unlocked the display case. She carefully removed the map and set it on top of the case. The three huddled together for a closer look.

"Do you know when . . . this map was created?" Evey asked.

"It may have a date by the legend," Professor Paulsen said.

"The what?" Archer asked.

"This thing with the little pictures," Evey said, pointing to the bottom right corner of the map. "It explains what the . . . symbols on the map mean. And it shows the . . . scale, which is how you tell distance on a map. An inch on this map represents . . . half a mile."

"Very impressive, Ms. Evey," Professor Paulsen said. "And the legend should also have . . ." she adjusted her glasses and looked more closely at the map. "Excellent! It says here the map was created in 1850."

Archer looked at the date. "Am I the only person who doesn't know maps? Is this like a cool, new trend I'm missing out on?"

Evey rolled her eyes. *If only it was a cool trend*, she thought. She turned to Professor Paulsen. "1850 is the . . . same time as the Coyote Pirate, right?"

"Yes," Professor Paulsen said. "That's right before he started attacking—or should I say, scaring ships. Now, let's see if your Coyote Bay is on here."

Evey pointed to the center of the map. "This is the area we were talking about. This looks like Apple Bay, so Turtle Lake . . . should be just . . . south of it. But instead of the lake, there's a bay to the . . . south. I've seen a lot of maps of Door County—"

"Probably millions," Archer said with a smirk.

Evey tried to hide a laugh. "I know Turtle Lake should be where this bay is. My grandpa . . . thought it could be because Lake Michigan's . . . water level dropped."

Professor Paulsen nodded. "I think you're right," she said. "How about that. I've walked by this map a hundred times and never noticed that. Let me find a new map to compare."

Professor Paulsen hurried out of the room. After a minute, she returned with a modern map and laid it next to the old one.

"No question," Archer said. "The mystery bay is definitely where Turtle Lake should be. Does the old map label the bay?"

Professor Paulsen pulled out a small magnifying glass. "Let's see."

After briefly looking through the magnifying glass, Professor Paulsen handed it to Evey and pointed to a spot in the middle of the bay. "I think the name is written there, but my eyes are not as good as they used to be. You try."

Evey grabbed the magnifying glass and looked at the spot Professor Paulsen pointed to. She saw a small, faded inscription.

"What does it say?" Archer asked.

Evey squinted to make out the letters. "Looks like . . . Coyote Bay!"

"No way! Let me see!" Archer took a turn reading the map with the magnifying glass. "That's it, alright," he said. "I wonder how it became a lake. Do you think it was just the water level changing like your grandpa said?"

Professor Paulsen turned to Evey. "Are you sure they didn't mention anything about this in the books you read?"

Evey shook her head no. "I don't think . . . they talked much about lakes."

Archer's eyes lit up. "Wait! Wasn't there a book about Door County's lakes and rivers in the gift shop?"

"I believe so," Professor Paulsen said. "Let's check."

The three left the nautical room and entered the gift shop behind the foyer. Archer ran to the bookshelf and grabbed a large book. "This one—*Waters of Door County*," he said.

Professor Paulsen studied the book. "Excellent," she said. "This should definitely help. It talks a lot about wildlife and fishing, but it covers the history of the lakes around here too." She handed the book back to Archer. "See what you can find on Turtle Lake while I start locking up."

Archer reviewed the table of contents to find the section on Turtle Lake, then read it aloud:

Turtle Lake is a large, inland lake in eastern Door County. Located next to Apple Bay, it is a popular destination for water activities including sailing, kayaking, and water skiing. Fishing is popular as well since the lake is home to abundant Bass, Northern Pike, and Walleye. The lake covers 1,100 acres. It is a shallow lake with an average depth of 7 feet.

The lake's source is the spring-fed Emerson Creek. A bridge divides the lake into northern and southern sections. The shallower northern section is surrounded by a large wetland that is designated a state nature preserve. The wetland is home to large populations of cranes and waterfowl, as well as many types of small mammals and turtles. The larger and deeper southern section is largely residential.

Turtle Lake was created by the townspeople of Apple Bay around 1870. Under the leadership of prominent citizen Margaret Andersen, the village oversaw a development project to make the lake an attractive tourist location. This included building a dam on the southeastern end to drain the marshy wetland there. The village also built the bridge across the northern end to improve access to the area.

The exact origin of the name Turtle Lake is unknown. However, oral histories refer to a large number of painted turtles in the area around the time of development. Prior to this time, the lake was actually a shallow bay . . .

"That's it!" Archer yelled.

Evey nodded. "There's more," she said.

. . . with a narrow channel running from its southeast corner into Lake Michigan. In the mid-nineteenth century, lumber ships traveled in-and-out of the bay for logging. However, by 1865, a drop in Lake Michigan's water level turned the entrance to the bay into a marshy wetland too shallow for most ships.

"Your grandpa was right," Archer said. "It was a drop in Lake Michigan's water level."

Evey smiled. "And now we know for . . . sure that Turtle Lake was . . . Coyote Bay."

"Did you find something?" Professor Paulsen asked as she walked into the room.

"We got it!" Archer said. "Coyote Bay did turn into Turtle Lake. The book agrees!"

Professor Paulsen put her glasses on and reviewed the page. "Excellent work you two. Truly great research. You should be proud of yourselves."

"No time to be proud," Archer said. Evey and Professor Paulsen looked at him. "We're not done yet, right?" he said. "We have to figure out where the lighthouse is. Have either of you ever seen one around Turtle Lake?"

Evey shook her head no.

"Me either," Professor Paulsen said. "But that doesn't mean there wasn't one in the past."

"Professor," Evey said, "shouldn't the old map . . . show lighthouses?"

"If it's a proper nautical chart it certainly should. Let's find out." The three returned to the nautical room and huddled around the old map again. "The legend should show us," Professor Paulsen said as she looked through her magnifying glass. "Here it is. According to the legend, lighthouses are marked with a teardrop shape."

"Everybody search the map for little teardrops," Archer said.

The three carefully looked over the map for the symbol. Professor Paulsen used the magnifying glass. "I don't see anything by the entrance to the bay," she said. "That's where a lighthouse would usually be."

"I found it!" Archer said. "Look over here." He pointed to a teardrop in the center of Coyote Bay. "That's weird—it's in the middle of the bay."

"It has an outline around it," Evey said. "Looks like a . . . small island."

Evey and Archer looked at each other. "The island!" they shouted at the same time. Their smiles turned to frowns.

"What's wrong?" Professor Paulsen asked.

Archer sighed. "Let's just say getting on that island isn't exactly easy. There are some kids who seem to think they own it."

"I see. That does sound problematic," Professor Paulsen said.

"Whenever kids go near the island, the East Siders throw them off—or worse."

"East Siders?"

"That's what we call them," Archer said. "They live on the east side of the lake."

"Have you told your parents about them?"

Archer recoiled. "No way! I can't have my parents involved. Then it becomes a whole thing." Archer frantically waved his arms in front of him like he was trying to swat a fly. "Then we would be the kids who went crying to our parents."

Professor Paulsen sat down on a nearby stool. "There's something to be said for trying to solve problems on your own. I can appreciate that, but remember, you're only kids. You should probably at least ask your parents for advice on this. Evey, what do you think?"

Evey bit her lip. *Ask my parents?* she thought. *And have them tell me to figure it out myself? No thanks! I would rather—*

"Evey," Professor Paulsen said, "is something upsetting you?"

Evey's jaw felt locked shut.

"Evey?" Archer said.

Evey's face turned red as Professor Paulsen and Archer stared at her. *Stop biting your lip!* she thought. *Just say something!* She grabbed her jaw and forced it open.

"What is it, dear?" Professor Paulsen said.

"I'm dine!" Evey shouted. She took a deep breath. "Fine."

Archer and Professor Paulsen stood quietly.

"Tarry," Evey mumbled. She sighed and rubbed her temples.

"That's okay," Professor Paulsen said. "In that case, just don't be afraid to ask for help if you need it. Fair enough?"

Evey and Archer nodded.

"Even if we can get by these kids," Archer said, "how do we find the lighthouse? That island is a jungle. It would take forever to search it."

"Perhaps the map can help," Professor Paulsen said. "The lighthouse looked like it was right in the middle of the island."

Evey looked at the map again. "I see a . . . problem."

"Now what?" Archer said. "My brain is on overload."

Evey pointed to the island in Coyote Bay. "Look how . . . different Coyote Bay and Turtle Lake are. Like my grandpa said, if the . . . water goes down, things . . . that were . . . underwater are dry now."

Archer looked at the maps. "What's your point?"

"The island . . . should be bigger now."

"Evey's right," Professor Paulsen said. "When the water level dropped, more of the island would have been exposed."

"I get it now," Archer said. "That's a bummer."

Professor Paulsen checked her watch. "Oh my, it's late. You two should be off so I can finish closing up."

"But Professor!" Archer protested. "How do we find an old lighthouse on a giant jungle island guarded by a group of obnoxious kids?"

Professor Paulsen stopped and smiled. "So far, you two have found almost everything on your own. I think you can figure this one out. Let me print copies of these maps for you. If there is any remnant of that lighthouse, I'm sure you can find it."

Evey and Archer nodded, then headed to the front door. In a couple of minutes, Professor Paulsen returned with the copies. Evey and Archer thanked her, said goodbye, and grabbed their helmets and bikes.

"What do you think, Evey?" Archer asked as he started pedaling. "We could search that island for days and not find anything. Do you have any super map skills that can help us?"

Evey stopped her bike. *Funny you ask, because I just got an idea,* she thought.

"What are you doing?" Archer said.

Evey turned her bike around. "We need to go to the . . . library."

CHAPTER 15

Evey and Archer raced their bikes to the library. With no traffic, they made it in only five minutes. Evey appreciated the empty streets. The next day, she knew thousands of tourists would arrive in Apple Bay for the Fourth of July holiday.

Evey and Archer set their bikes by a tree. "Why exactly did we race here?" Archer asked as he put his hands on his knees and took several deep breaths.

"I think I can . . . find it—the light . . . house," Evey said. She started jogging toward the door.

"Wait up," Archer said as he wiped the sweat from his forehead. "Aren't you tired after that?"

Evey shrugged. *Cross country is good for something*, she thought. She waited for Archer to catch his breath, then the two entered the building. They waved to the librarian at the checkout desk, then put two seats together next to one of the computers. Evey opened a browser and loaded a mapping website. She switched the image to satellite so it showed actual overhead pictures of the area. She scrolled around and zoomed in until the image centered above Turtle Lake.

"My dad showed me this website to . . . plan my runs," Evey said.

"How close can it zoom?" Archer asked. Evey zoomed in until Coyote Island took up the entire screen. "Apparently, super close," Archer said. "You can see individual trees and everything."

Evey leaned closer to the screen. "Let's see if anything looks like a light . . . house."

"Or a pile of scrap," Archer said. "I can't imagine there's much left."

The two searched every inch of the screen. After a few minutes, they leaned back into their chairs. Evey rubbed her temples.

"Just a bunch of trees," Archer said. "That place really is a jungle. At least it's pretty. This picture must have been taken in the fall. Look at the orange and red leaves. It might be better to have a picture in the winter. With the leaves gone, you could see more, but I guess snow could cover . . ."

Evey sat quietly, staring at the screen. *Tall grass*, she thought. She touched her cheek as she remembered the grass slapping her as she ran from the coyotes in her vision.

"Sorry, I'm rambling again," Archer said. "What are you thinking about, Evey?"

"This oval-shaped area," she said as she pointed to a green patch in the center of the island.

Archer leaned forward. "Okay, what are we looking at?"

"The orange and red areas are trees. The oval area is all green. It . . . has to be a grassy clearing of . . . some sort."

"I like grass. It's easy to walk on. I don't like mowing it though. Do you know my uncle doesn't have grass? He has clover in his yard, and he says he barely ever has to—"

Evey raised her eyebrow.

"Sorry," Archer said. "I'm still worked up from that bike ride. I don't think I've ever ridden that fast."

Evey pointed back to the screen. "In my . . . vision, the entire island was covered in long grass. There was only one tree. So, maybe . . . this clearing is the original part of the island."

Archer scratched his neck. "I don't know. It's been over a hundred years since the water level dropped. Who knows what could've changed on that island. I wish there was a way to be certain."

"Maybe there is," Evey said while digging in her backpack. She pulled out the maps from Professor Paulsen and spread them out on a nearby table. She put the newer map down first, then laid the old map with Coyote Bay on top of it.

"What are you doing?" Archer asked.

"I'm using the old map that . . . shows where the . . . lighthouse is to mark the . . . matching location on the new map."

"Sounds complicated."

"These maps use the same . . . scale," Evey said. "The distances . . . should match. I'm going to line up the Apple Bay Marina on both maps. I know it was in the . . . same location back . . . then, because it was built in 1850."

"How do you know that?" Archer asked.

"It's on a plaque I . . . saw there."

Archer folded his arms. "That seems really convenient you happened to learn that random and important fact, but continue."

Evey shrugged and continued adjusting the maps. "If we line these up . . . using the marina, then the island . . . should line up too. We can put a pencil on the light . . . house on the old map, and push it through so it . . . marks its location on the new map."

"That's really smart," Archer said. "Where did you come up with that?"

"I just . . . thought of it," Evey said.

"Apparently, you do have super map skills."

Evey shrugged. *I'm just happy my map knowledge was actually useful,* she thought.

"Is your bedroom at home covered with maps of the world?" Archer asked.

Evey sighed. "Yes, I have a few maps on . . . my wall."

"Ha! I was right!" Archer pumped his fist.

"Shush!" Evey said.

"What? Nobody's here. It's not like . . ." Archer paused as his eyes wandered to the library's foyer, ". . . Finn is standing over there staring at us."

Evey rolled her eyes. "Funny," she grumbled.

"Actually, I'm not joking this time. Finn is literally at the checkout desk, staring at us."

Evey turned to look. *What!* she screamed in her thoughts.

Finn leaned his back against the desk with his arms crossed. His messy hair covered his right eye, but Evey could see his other eye looking directly at her. She stared back with her mouth open in shock. Archer awkwardly waved. Finn stared back, his face completely still. Suddenly, he turned away, snatched a pile of books from the checkout desk, and hurriedly walked out the door.

"That was odd and unexpected," Archer said.

Evey ignored him as her mind flooded with worries. *Did Finn hear us?* she thought. *How long was he there? Did he see my maps? Did he—*

"Nothing like a Finn sighting to ruin the mood," Archer said. "Although, seeing him here adds a new dimension to his character. I feel like the library is not a typical bully hangout. And did you see how big his pile of books was? Is he studying to be a yacht captain, or maybe—"

"Archer," Evey said sternly. "He night dav durd—no . . . heard us!"

"I guess," Archer said, "but what's he going to do—kidnap and torture us until we tell him what we know?"

Evey took a deep breath and rubbed her temples. *I guess Archer's right*, she thought. *Hannah already told Finn we're looking for something in the lake, so it doesn't matter.* Evey looked at Archer. "Yea," she said. "It's . . . probably . . . fine."

Archer nodded. "Besides, he doesn't look so tough without his friends. Did you see how quick he ran out of here?"

Evey shrugged.

"Anyway, where were we?" Archer asked.

"Maps," Evey said.

"That's right! Do you know how I can tell you really love maps?"

Evey raised her eyebrow.

Archer smiled. "When you talk about map stuff," he said, "you say a lot more than usual, and you don't even pause that much."

Evey lowered her eyebrow and tilted her head to the side. *Wait—what? Is he right? What does that mean if—*

120

"Everybody has their weird things," Archer continued, cutting off Evey's train of thought. "I collect paintings of video game characters, and I don't even play video games anymore. I'm too obsessed with badminton. Which reminds me, I need to practice more if—"

"Archer, focus!"

"Sorry! Maps-maps-maps—Turtle Lake—lighthouse. Let's do this."

Evey finished adjusting the maps to line up the marina. "Hold the apps . . . maps, I mean," she said. "Keep them . . . together so . . . they don't . . . move." *Ugh! Now I can't stop paying attention to how I'm talking.*

"Ready," Archer said as he pressed the maps together.

Evey pushed the pencil on the lighthouse until it poked through the old map copy and marked the new map underneath.

"Let's see if it worked," Archer said as he moved the old map out of the way. On the new map, the pencil left a dot near the center of Coyote Island. "It's not 'X marks the spot,' but I think it'll work!"

"The dot is in the . . . island's center," Evey said. "So, the . . . light . . . house has to be in the . . . clearing."

"Awesome, but that brings up another question—how do we find the clearing? We could easily get lost in that jungle."

Evey sat back in her chair to think. She replayed her experience on the island. "I know there is . . . there's a trail," she said.

"Where?" Archer asked.

"It goes from the beach to . . . the cliff."

"There's a cliff on this place?"

121

"It's the area the East Siders . . . threw me off. The big rock . . . wall. That's what . . . they call it."

"Oh, I get it," Archer said. "That's pretty funny."

Evey raised her eyebrow.

"Not funny that they threw you in," Archer said. "Just its name—um—anyway, can you see the cliff on the map?"

Evey looked at the computer screen. "I think it's . . . this thin line," she said, pointing to a gray patch along the west side of the island. "Why?"

"Because if we get chased by the East Siders, I want to avoid that."

"I think we can . . . use it."

"I hope for something other than jumping off."

Evey smiled. "Look at the screen," she said. Archer leaned forward while Evey pointed to the clearing. "The clearing is . . . far from the boat landing." She used the website to draw a line from the rocky beach on the north end of the island to the grassy clearing. It measured over half a mile.

Archer frowned. "Half a mile of hiking in that mess doesn't sound fun."

Evey drew another line on the computer from the cliff to the clearing. "But the cliff is only a few . . . hundred feet . . . west of it," she said. "If we take the trail to the . . . the cliff, we'll be close."

"Sounds like a plan to me. Just bring some weapons in case we get attacked by a mountain lion."

"What?" Evey blurted out before she could move her eyebrow.

"They're terrifying!" Archer said. "I went to Montana with my family once. There were signs everywhere warning of this angry mountain lion—or cougar—I think they're the same thing. Anyway, this thing kept attacking hikers in the park we stayed at."

"I don't . . . think there are . . . mountain lions in . . . Door County."

"I'm just saying, who knows what's on that island. Mosquitoes too. It's probably covered with mosquitoes. Bring the bug spray, and—sorry, I'm rambling again."

Evey shook her head. *I'm more worried about coyotes*, she thought.

"Hi kids," the librarian interrupted. "We have to close now. Can you finish up your work?"

Evey and Archer nodded. Evey packed the maps in her backpack and the two left the library and grabbed their bikes.

"How are your sailing lessons?" Archer asked. "Are you going to be ready to sail to Coyote Island?"

Evey nodded. "Tomorrow is my . . . last lesson," she said. She stopped walking her bike and turned to Archer. "Any chance you . . . do you . . . want to . . . come? It would be goo—I mean . . ." Evey paused and took a deep breath. *Get it together!* she thought. *I'm not asking him on a date!* "It would be good," she continued, "if you knew . . . about the boat."

"I did plan on some hardcore badminton practice tomorrow, but I think I can squeeze you in," Archer said.

Evey chuckled. "We can pick you up . . . around 8:30."

"Okay."

Evey started to pedal, then stopped. "Ugh! I . . . forgot!" she said.

"Forgot what?" Archer asked.

"My teacher—Hannah—she's nice, but she . . . Finn's sister."

"What!" Archer yelled. "How did you not tell me that?"

Evey shrugged.

"I'm surprised she agreed to teach you," Archer said.

"She's really nice—nothing like . . . Finn," Evey said. "I ran into . . . them at Chester's."

"Talk about awkward."

"Worse yet, Hannah told Finn I'm learning to . . . sail and looking for a . . . a treasure."

Archer scratched his neck. "Great, he'll never let us near the island now."

"I know," Evey said.

"Although," Archer said, "this could actually be a great opportunity. Maybe we can use Hannah to get some information on Finn."

Evey raised her eyebrow.

"You know," Archer said, "like find out more about the East Siders—like when they'll be gone so we can explore the island."

"That's actually a . . . great idea," Evey said.

"Of course it is. I got it from a spy movie."

Evey laughed. *Maybe I should spend less time looking at maps and start watching more movies*, she thought.

"This will be awesome," Archer said. "Tomorrow morning we'll find the East Siders' secret weakness. They'll never see us coming!"

Evey high-fived Archer. *Maybe we can do this after all,* she thought.

CHAPTER 16

Friday morning, Grandpa drove Evey and Archer to the marina for her last sailing lesson. He told Evey he needed to run some last-minute errands before their family arrived the next day, so Archer's parents agreed to pick them up.

"Morning, Evey!" Hannah said once she saw Evey and Archer coming down the dock. "I see you brought a friend today."

"Hi, I'm Archer," he said.

"Is it alright if . . . Archer comes?" Evey asked.

"No problem at all," Hannah said. "It's going to be a big day. For your last lesson, you're going to sail all the way to Blueberry Island."

Evey forced a smile to stop herself from biting her lip.

"You'll be fine," Hannah said. "I know it's a further trip than usual. Just take some extra time reviewing your chart so you know the area."

Evey looked at the flagpoles at the end of the marina. The flags flapped in the strong wind. *A little too breezy for my liking,* she thought.

"Whoa, it looks choppy out there," Archer said as he pointed at the lake. "See those waves, Evey?"

Evey bit her lip. *Not cool, Archer!* she thought.

"Let's get going," Hannah said. "In the boat, you two."

Evey took some deep breaths as she climbed into the boat. She put her life vest on and looked over a chart to figure out a course. Blueberry Island sat about four miles to the northeast. It was a small island, but further away than anything Evey previously sailed to. She finished plotting her course and gave it to Hannah.

Hannah took a minute to review Evey's work, then handed the chart back. "This looks good," she said.

Evey put the chart away and started prepping the lines. *Stop biting your lip!* she thought when she tasted a little blood.

"Evey," Hannah said, "how about you play teacher today. I find that talking about what you're doing helps distract you. Take Archer through all the steps of setting up the boat and working the sails. You can even have him help control the jib sail or the rudder."

Evey nodded, then motioned for Archer to sit next to her. She talked him through each step as she readied the sails. Next, she demonstrated how to adjust the jib sail and duck under the boom while moving it back-and-forth. After explaining the rigging, she removed the dock lines and steered the sailboat toward the bay.

The waves grew as soon as they cleared the marina. Evey stayed focused by telling Archer how to steer with the rudder, as well as when and how to adjust the sails. Once they reached a steady course toward Blueberry Island, she leaned back onto the trampoline between the rudder and boom to relax.

Hannah checked the lines and sails to make sure Evey set everything correctly. "Looks good," she said. "I told you it helps to talk everything out."

Evey smiled.

Archer moved to one of the small benches on the port side of the boat to sit near Hannah. "So, Hannah," he said, "Evey told me your family lives on Turtle Lake, and you have a brother around our age." He winked at Evey.

I hope that spy movie taught him how to be subtle, she thought.

"That's right," Hannah said to Archer. "Finn—have you met him?"

"Just once, very briefly," Archer said. "He and his friends always seem to be out on their boat, or on the island."

"That's my brother and his friends, alright. They spend all summer out there. They even camp there a lot of nights."

"Are they ever not there?"

"My parents make him come home now and then. Honestly, I don't understand the attraction of that place. I went there with him once. It's nothing but trees and mosquitoes."

"And mountain lions," Evey whispered to Archer, making him laugh.

"What's that?" Hannah asked.

"Nothing," Archer said. "So, is that Finn's sailboat they use? It's really cool."

"It's his—well, ours, technically," Hannah said. "It was my parents', but they bought a new one two years ago, so they gave that one to us. But I don't use it too much since I sail all day."

"Did you teach Finn to sail?"

127

"No, my parents taught us both, but Finn didn't really take to it until recently. He's gotten a lot better, but he still has a tendency to push the boat too hard."

Evey smirked. *Pushes the boat too hard—sounds like a weakness,* she thought. *Apparently, it was a good spy movie.*

"What about the Fourth of July?" Archer asked. "Do you take the boat out, then? I bet it would be cool to watch the fireworks from the lake."

"We usually have a party with some of our neighbors," Hannah said. "We watch the fireworks from our dock. I think Finn and his friends are planning on watching from the island, so he'll probably take the boat out."

Evey and Archer exchanged frowns.

"Does your family ever take the boat on vacation?" Archer asked. "I bet it would be cool to sail it in the Great Lakes."

"No, the boat stays in Turtle Lake," Hannah said. "But we usually go to Canada in the summer to see my grandparents. In fact, I think we're leaving in a few weeks."

Evey perked up. *If they go to Canada, we can explore the island!* she thought. She squeezed her fingers. *For someone who doesn't think before talking, Archer is really good at this.*

"Canada—that sounds cool," Archer said while winking at Evey. "Is that a long trip?"

"About a week," Hannah said. "My grandparents live in a town not too far from Detroit. We take a ferry to Michigan, then drive the rest of the way."

Evey felt the boat slow. She looked at the flag on top of the mast and saw that the wind had shifted. It now came from the northeast, almost directly in front of them. She

128

shifted the boom to adjust the sails, then steered the boat north.

Hannah gave Evey a thumbs up. "I was just about to say you should check the wind. Great job!"

Evey smiled.

"Where are we going?" Archer asked. "Isn't the island in the other direction?"

"Do you want to tell him, Evey?" Hannah asked.

"We're tacking," Evey said. "The wind changed so it . . . was blowing . . . straight at us. We can't . . . sail into that. I have to keep turning. Go north, east . . . then north again."

"Evey's become quite the pro at tacking," Hannah said. "It seems we're always sailing into the wind together, doesn't it?"

Evey nodded.

"Time to double check your surroundings, though," Hannah said. "Make sure your new course is clear."

Evey took the binoculars out of the storage box attached to the mast. She scanned the area to follow her new, zig zag course.

Archer put his hands above his eyes and looked in the same direction. "See anything?" he asked.

"Some boats by a beach to the left—or . . . port side," Evey said. "Nothing is in the—wait, Hannah, I see a . . . warning buoy. It has a . . . diamond . . . shape on it. That means . . . rocks, right?"

"Let me see," Hannah said. She took the binoculars and looked at the spot. "You're right, those are definitely rocks. That's why you always have to keep checking your surroundings. You never know what might be ahead— especially when you change your course."

Evey worked the boom and rudder, then directed Archer to help adjust the sails. Together, they turned the boat to the east to move further from the rocks.

Archer turned to Hannah. "We shouldn't have to worry about these things on Turtle Lake, right?"

Hannah put her hands on her hips.

"What?" Archer said. "Turtle Lake is so shallow, it's basically a giant pool."

"Turtle Lake may be shallow," Hannah said, "but don't you think for a minute you can sail out there without being prepared. There are rocky areas that can damage a boat, and when the wind picks up, the waves can still be pretty rough."

"Okay, I get it," Archer said. "Never underestimate anything. It's like this one time my dad asked me if I wanted to hike up this big hill. I was all excited and like 'no problem!' But when we got there, I saw this thing and I started to . . ."

Evey zoned out of Archer's story as she steered the boat to the north again, making sure to keep the rocks out of her path. She could see Blueberry Island clearly now. It was a tiny patch of land covered in rocks and seagulls. Looking at it gave Evey an urge to grab her grandma's crystal. She took it out from beneath her shirt and held it in the sun, making it sparkle.

Why does this place look so familiar? Evey thought. *I know I've never been—wait—why do I feel sleepy?*

Everything around Evey darkened. Archer and Hannah's voices faded away. Storm clouds appeared and a strong rain poured down on her. The waves rocked the boat back-and-forth. Cold water splashed Evey's face, nearly knocking her over. She wiped the water from her eyes and steadied herself on a large, wooden steering wheel.

Where did this giant wheel come from? Evey thought. *What happened to the little rudder? What happened to the little boat?* Looking around, Evey realized she was no longer on the catamaran with Archer and Hannah, but alone on a much larger, old-fashioned sailing ship. *What's happening!* she thought.

Boom! Evey heard a rumble followed by a whistling sound. She turned around and froze. A hundred feet behind her, a huge, wooden sailboat plowed through the waves. Evey saw dozens of men scurrying around the boat and working the sails. It was quickly gaining on her.

Boom! Evey saw a flash and puff of smoke.

They're shooting at me! she thought. *Are you kidding me! Send me back to the grassy island with the coyotes!* Evey looked around for a way to escape. A small island sat off her starboard side. *Is that Blueberry—wait, then where are the—* Evey looked ahead and saw a field of dark objects in the water. *The rocks!*

Evey turned the wheel as fast as she could, moving the boat to port. She took a deep breath as she watched the rocks narrowly pass her starboard side.

Boom! Another cannon blast from the ship sent a shot splashing into the water off the side of Evey's boat. She turned and saw that the chasing boat was much closer now, but it did not turn as quickly as she did.

Crack! A thunderous snapping of wood sounded through the air as the large boat smashed against the rocks. Men fell from the sails. Pieces of the boat broke away as it crashed on its side.

"Evey," Archer said.

"What?" she replied, snapping out of her daze.

"You zoned out for a few seconds."

"Uh . . . I was just tearing . . . staring . . . at the island."

"Try not to daydream when you're on the water," Hannah said.

Evey nodded. She looked at her surroundings. The sky was clear and Blueberry Island sat just ahead. *What's going on?* she thought. *Was that another vision? Was it related to the Coyote Pirate? Wait, didn't I read about something like that?*

"We're here!" Hannah said. "You made it to Blueberry Island, Evey. Nice work!"

"Uh . . . cool," Evey said. She shook her head a few times to wake herself up, then watched the steady stream of seagulls landing on and taking off from the island.

"That's it?" Archer asked. "Doesn't look like much of an island. Shouldn't there be some blueberry bushes on there or something?"

"No blueberries," Hannah said. "It's mainly rocks and bird poop. The first time I sailed here, I made the mistake of docking and walking around. I had to dodge the seagulls."

Archer laughed while Evey stared at the island. *Something tells me this place's history is a little more interesting,* she thought.

"There are plenty of cool islands around Door County," Hannah said, "but this is definitely not one of them. And I have no idea where the name comes from. It makes a convenient destination for sailing lessons, though."

After they reached the other side of the island, Evey let Archer control the rudder while she plotted the trip back to the marina. Sailing with the wind behind them, they made it back to the marina quickly. Once they docked, Hannah left Evey to take care of the sails and lines while she went to the office.

When Hannah was out of sight, Archer leaned over. "Something tells me there was more to your daydream than you said. You looked spooked."

Evey nodded. "I had another . . . vision. It reminded me of . . . something I read."

"What was it?"

"I was on a big . . . sailboat in a torm—I mean . . . storm. This huge . . . ship was . . . chasing—"

"Were they zombies?" Archer interrupted.

Evey raised her eyebrow.

"Stop with the eyebrow, Evey. You're communicating with a dead pirate. I'm telling you, zombies are showing up eventually."

Evey rolled her eyes. "They—the . . . humans—were . . . shooting at me!"

"Yikes," Archer said. "I think that's scarier than zombies."

"I know," Evey said. "I had to . . . steer around rocks, then the big . . . ship . . . crashed."

"What does that have to do with the Coyote Pirate?"

"I read that he . . . he wrecked a few . . . ships that chased him. He led . . . them into . . . shallow and rocky . . . waters."

Archer put his finger to his lips to shush Evey as Hannah walked down the dock.

"Hey Evey," Hannah said, "it looks like you put everything away properly." She hopped onto the boat and inspected the sails and ropes. "I have good news—you officially passed!" Hannah and Archer clapped, then Hannah handed Evey a piece of paper. "Here's your certificate. You are now officially a certified junior sailor. Congratulations!"

Evey smiled as she looked at her certificate. *Sweet*, she thought, *something other than maps to hang in my bedroom.*

"Just promise me something when you're out there on Turtle Lake," Hannah said.

"Yea?" Evey said.

"Always be prepared—life vest, radio or phone, check the weather, tell somebody where you're going and when you expect to be back, and most importantly . . ." Hannah motioned for Evey to finish.

"Know your . . . surroundings," Evey said.

Hannah clapped. "Perfect!"

As Evey and Archer said thank you and goodbye to Hannah, Archer's parents pulled into the marina parking lot.

"Time to go," Archer said. "This is great—you know how to sail, and now we know that Finn is leaving for a week soon. That means no boat for the other East Siders. We need to make sure we're in Door County when he's gone."

"How do we know . . . when?" Evey asked.

"We use spies," Archer said in his deep voice.

Evey raised her eyebrow.

"You know, like lookouts. Your grandpa will be here, and somebody's almost always at my family's place. We can have them watch for us. Once the East Siders are gone, we come back, find the lighthouse, and the secret is ours!"

CHAPTER 17

Evey hopped out of Archer's parents' car, said thanks, and jogged down Grandpa's driveway. Hearing his radio, she ran to the garage, but skidded to a stop when she noticed that the sailboat was missing.

"Grandpa," Evey said.

Grandpa turned around from his work bench. "I've got a surprise for you," he said with a big smile.

Evey raised her eyebrow.

"I may have been fibbing a little earlier," Grandpa said. "That errand I needed to run was at the Adventure Store."

Evey squeezed her fingers. *The sails!* she thought.

"Down by the lake," Grandpa said.

Evey sprinted across the long yard to the dock. She saw the sailboat sitting in the grass, with both the new mainsail and jib fluttering slightly in the breeze. Their bright colors changed from yellow and orange at the bottom, to red, pink, and purple at the top. The mainsail stretched nearly twenty feet high. Evey turned her attention to the rest of the sailboat. The repaired hulls looked brand new. The white paint and red streaks shined in the sunlight. She took her shoes off and stretched out on the trampoline as if in a hammock.

"Comfy?" Grandpa asked as he strolled down the yard.

Evey nodded.

Grandpa rested his hand on the mast. "What do you think?"

Evey's face froze in a smile. *It's awesome,* she thought. *As in better than all the pie and ice cream in Door County.*

"I take it that smile means you're happy," Grandpa said. "What are you sitting around for? Test the sails."

Evey practiced lowering and raising the sails, and maneuvering the boom. After finishing, she motioned to the lake. "Can we?" she asked Grandpa.

"Of course!" he said.

Evey hopped off the boat and grabbed one of the hulls.

"Not so fast," Grandpa said. "Remember your lessons. We need our supplies, even for a quick spin. I already put a chart in the boat, but we need life vests."

Evey nodded and ran to the shed. She grabbed two life vests and raced back to the dock. She and Grandpa put the vests on and lugged the boat to the shore. They carefully set it in the water, then stepped on. Together, they pushed the boat away from the dock. Once clear, Evey raised the two sails. They immediately caught the wind, pulling the boat forward.

"Where to?" Grandpa asked as he took control of the rudder handle. He handed Evey the chart.

"Uh . . ." she replied.

"All this time worrying about fixing the boat and you never thought of where you want to take it?"

Evey shrugged. *I guess we could go to Coyote Island,* she thought. *That's assuming Grandpa wants to stand guard for a few hours while I search for a ruined lighthouse. I wonder if he would throw the East Siders off the cliff for me?*

"We could circle the lake," Grandpa said. "Or, what about Grandma's notes? Anywhere she wrote about that you want to go?"

Evey remembered an entry from the notebook. "Yes!" she said. "The east—no . . . southeast part of the lake. Grandma wrote about . . . seeing turtles near a . . . shallow area."

"That's more like it. Where is this shallow spot?"

"Grandma said she . . . kayaked east to a cove, ten—I mean . . . then . . . went south. She said it was near a big . . . yard."

"That sounds like your grandma. She never was very specific with directions. Let's see if we can find this spot. East we go."

Evey reviewed the chart, then adjusted the sails to head toward the eastern shore. The boat began to rock a little as they moved further into the lake. The wind was light, but strong enough to make small waves. Evey dipped her hand in the water. It felt very cool compared to the warm air. Grandpa dug his hand in and splashed Evey.

"Hey!" she shouted. She returned the splash with one of her own. After a few more shots, both of them were soaked. They laughed, called a truce, and stretched their feet out to relax on the trampoline.

"I sure wish your grandma could see this," Grandpa said. "She was so excited to buy this boat."

Evey noticed Grandpa's eyes watering. She leaned on his shoulder. "Grandpa, when . . . was the first time you and Grandma came . . . here?"

Grandpa rubbed his eyes. "Let's see. That would be right after we got married, so about forty-five years ago. But I'd been up a bunch before that."

"What was it like . . . then?" Evey asked.

"Not much different, to be honest."

Evey raised her eyebrow.

"What I mean is," Grandpa continued, "when I was a kid, I did the same stuff up here that you do now. We would go to the beach, waterski, mini-golf, eat ice cream, play a bunch of ping-pong."

"My dad said you once . . . water . . . skied from Cherry Bay to Eagle Island."

Grandpa put his hands behind his head and winked. "That was a long time ago."

Evey smiled. "Why did you and Grandma . . . want to live up . . . here?"

"I think it's mainly just how slow it is here. Back in Illinois, it seemed we could never find much quality time with each other. But here, we could fill an entire day working in the garden and making dinner together. We knew the house would make a perfect vacation home, and we figured we could eventually retire here too. I just wish your grandma lived long enough to be here full-time, like me."

Grandpa paused and rubbed his eyes. "And you kids and your parents were a big part of it," he continued. "Grandma wanted the house to be a place for her entire family. How did she put it?" Grandpa rubbed his chin. "That's it—she said she wanted a place where her grandkids could be kids. Have a break from the pressure of growing up. Take time to pay attention to the fun stuff right in front of you. Door County is great for that. Like the lake today—look how beautiful it is."

Evey looked at the view surrounding the sailboat. A few white clouds dotted the blue sky. The sunlight reflected off the lake. Evey wrapped her arm around Grandpa's. *I think I get what you mean*, she thought.

"You know, Evey," Grandpa continued, "I'm really happy you stayed up here the last few weeks. It's been great spending so much time with you."

Evey's jaw felt locked. She rubbed it and took a deep breath. "Me . . . too," she mumbled.

After a few more minutes of sailing, Grandpa sat up. "There's the cove straight ahead. Now, let's see if we can find the big yard. South we go!"

Evey and Grandpa turned the boat to the south and followed the shoreline so they could search for the big yard. Evey pointed to an area ahead of them. "Maybe . . . there," she said.

"I do see a lot of grass," Grandpa said. He moved to the front of the boat while Evey took over the rudder. A large, white house, set far back from the water, came into view. "Oh, it's Blacksmith Mansion!" Grandpa said.

Evey raised her eyebrow.

"The house up there," Grandpa said. "It's called Blacksmith Mansion. They have weddings and parties there. I went there once with your grandma. It's a neat old place."

"Do you . . . think this is the . . . spot?" Evey asked.

"Could be—that certainly is a big yard," Grandpa said. He looked ahead of the boat. "And, it looks like the water is about to get pretty shallow, so I think we're on the right track."

Evey turned and saw a sandbar directly ahead. She jerked the rudder. The sudden turn threw her and Grandpa to the side.

"Hey! You trying to throw me off?" Grandpa said as he clung to the mast.

Evey looked down at the rudder handle. "Tarry, I wasn't heck—I mean . . . checking my . . . surroundings."

"You definitely do need to do that. But remember what Hannah showed you—in this boat, you can just lift the rudder and sail over something like that."

Evey rubbed her temples.

"Don't worry about it," Grandpa said. "Eventually, it will all become natural. It's like learning to ride a bike."

The sharp turn moved them closer to the shore. Evey dropped the sails to bring the boat to a stop.

Grandpa examined the yard. "This must be the place," he said.

Evey looked at the shore. She noticed some fallen tree trunks on the edge of the large yard that stuck into the water. She spotted three turtles sitting on one of them. "Turtles!" she yelled as she pointed them out to Grandpa.

"Ah ha! Success!" he said as he high-fived Evey.

"I guess Grandma's directions were . . . okay," Evey said.

"She had a way with those things," Grandpa said. "Congratulations on a successful first cruise, by the way."

Evey smiled, then turned back to the turtles. "I wish my dad was . . . here. He always complains he can't . . . find turtles."

"You'll have to bring him next time."

Evey watched the three turtles as they sat perfectly still on the log. *Are they dead?* she wondered. Finally, one slightly raised its head. "Although," Evey said, "I don't . . . understand why he likes turtles. They're . . . boring."

Grandpa laughed. "On that note, I guess it's time to head back. Can you do it on your own?"

Evey nodded and went to work maneuvering the boom and raising the sails. She turned the rudder to bring the boat around.

"Nice work," Grandpa said. "It looks like you're ready to be Captain Evey."

Evey gave Grandpa a thumbs up.

"You know," he said, "when your grandma and I bought this boat, we couldn't come up with a name for it. Have you thought about one?"

Evey nodded.

"Well?" Grandpa asked.

"Sunrise."

CHAPTER 18

Evey felt too excited to sleep that night. As soon as she and Grandpa finished their cruise, they had painted "Sunrise" on the boat's two hulls. Sitting in bed, Evey kept visualizing how the bold, red letters looked on the boat. She imagined sailing to Coyote Island to search for the lighthouse. Then, she wondered about the meaning of her vision during the sailing lesson. Questions raced through her mind.

What if my parents don't let me come back when the East Siders leave? Evey thought. *What if they do, but I can't find the lighthouse? What if it doesn't even exist anymore? What if I'm wrong about everything? What if the crystal brings the Coyote Pirate back to life and he tries to eat my brains? Ugh! I need to stop listening to Archer.*

Evey stared out the window to try to clear her mind. She fixed her gaze on the clouds until they moved aside to uncover the nearly full moon.

A familiar red light lit up the room. Evey turned toward the nightstand and saw her grandma's crystal glowing again. She hopped out of bed and grabbed it. She held it up to the window, making the glow brighten.

Ha! I wasn't hallucinating, Evey thought. *This thing really does glow.* She bit her lip. *Although, I might actually feel better if it wasn't real.*

With the crystal in hand, Evey's thoughts faded away and her body relaxed. She yawned as she tucked herself back into bed. She stared at the crystal, watching tiny red sparkles twirl around the center. Her eyes grew heavy. She closed them, but she could still see the red glow.

The warmth of Evey's bed melted away as a cold, wet chill crept over her. *This doesn't feel right,* she thought. *Unless Howie wet my bed earlier, and I just noticed it.*

Evey opened her eyes and sat up. Instead of her bedroom, she found herself on a pile of long, wet grass. A small lighthouse stood in front of her. *A lighthouse?* she thought. *The lighthouse? Is that it?* The wooden lighthouse was about as tall as a two-story house. It sat on a small hill with several boulders scattered around its base.

Wait a minute, Evey thought. *If the crystal is trying to help me, there's a reason I'm—*

A loud howl cut off Evey's train of thought. She jumped to her feet. *Not the coyotes again!* she thought. She turned around to face the source of the noise. Hidden in the long grass, she saw a pair of yellow eyes staring at her. Then a second, a third, and a fourth.

The yellow eyes lunged out of the grass and barked as they sprinted toward Evey. She turned and ran as fast as she could to the lighthouse. She reached for the door and pulled it open. She lunged inside and slammed the heavy, wood door shut just before the coyotes crashed against it.

The coyotes growled as they clawed at the door. Trembling, Evey fell to the ground and crawled to the opposite side of the room.

The growling and scratching faded away, but another sound caught Evey's attention. *What is that?* she thought as she listened to the quiet screeching. *Is that coming from beneath me?*

Evey looked at the wooden floorboards. They shook as if something was hitting them from underneath. The screeching grew louder until a hatch in the floor opened. Evey held her breath as a dark figure climbed out of the opening.

"Fancy meeting you again," the figure said.

Evey exhaled. *It's him—the Coyote Pirate*, she thought. Even though he held a lantern, Evey still could not see anything other than the outline of his boots, coat, and tricorn hat.

"I apologize," the Coyote Pirate said. "I see I've frightened you again. I promise that is not my intention."

Evey rubbed her jaw. "Coyote . . . Pirate," she mumbled.

"I see you've made some progress," he said. He pointed to the bright light above them. "And have you discovered what this is?"

"The . . . sun . . . sunrise." Evey continued to rub her jaw.

"Yes," the Coyote Pirate said.

Evey looked up. The light came from a lamp surrounded by a series of mirrors. *Look beneath the sunrise,* she thought.

Evey turned to the Coyote Pirate. "The . . . secret— beneath the . . . sunrise," she said. "Is that . . . what you're doing? Hiding it? It's like a nap—or . . . map."

The Coyote Pirate nodded. "Beyond the cellar, you'll find what you need. But I must apologize, for I cannot stay. Time is of the essence." He stood and reached for the door.

"Wait!" Evey yelled. "Why . . . why am I . . . here?"

The Coyote Pirate stopped and turned. "That, regretfully, I do not know. The crystal can offer guidance, but you already seem close to the secret. Perhaps there is something else you are struggling with."

Like losing my mind, Evey thought.

"I can assure you that is not the case," the Coyote Pirate said.

"How to you—I mean . . . do . . ." Evey tried to ask.

The Coyote Pirate pointed to the crystal around Evey's neck. She looked down at it. The crystal again glowed red as moonlight shined through a window.

Why don't I know what he's thinking—doesn't seem very fair, Evey thought. She let out a loud sigh and turned back to the Coyote Pirate. "I am tug . . . struggle. I don't . . . know if I can do this."

"You've already come so far," the Coyote Pirate said.

"But . . ." Evey's voice trailed off.

"But what?"

"It's mot up to nee!" Evey shouted. She rubbed her temples. "My parents and the . . . East Siders! I don't know if I can get on the land . . . island, much less find . . . sun . . . the . . . light . . . house. And I don't know if . . . this . . . if . . . is this even eel!" Evey rubbed her jaw. "I mean . . ."

"Real?" the Coyote Pirate asked.

Evey nodded.

"The secret is real."

"That's mot what I axed!" Evey shouted. "Am I alking to you? To your . . . your spirit? Is this some . . . vision . . . or memory? Or am I just . . . just . . . dreams!"

"I cannot answer that question," the Coyote Pirate said. "I myself don't fully understand the crystal. I don't think it can be understood. But I also don't think it needs to be."

Evey raised her eyebrow. *Great, he's going back to the riddles*, she thought.

"I see my answer does not satisfy you," the Coyote Pirate said. "In that case, I shall offer my own question." He leaned closer to Evey. "Does it matter if this is real?"

"Yes . . ." Evey stopped herself.

"The secret is out there," the Coyote Pirate said. "Whether you call our conversation a vision or dream does not change that."

"But why me? I'm just a id . . . kid. And I'm not . . . special. I'm not . . . smart. I'm not . . . not strong. I can't even peak—I mean seek—no, I . . ." Evey put her face in her hands and grunted.

The Coyote Pirate kneeled on the floor. "I am no one special, either."

"You're a . . . a . . . a legend!"

"Legends are often not what they seem. Find this lighthouse and you'll see for yourself."

Evey sighed. "This would be . . . easier if you . . . would just tell me the . . . secret."

The Coyote Pirate laughed. "Remember young lady, this is just a memory. And memories get a little—"

"Foggy," Evey cut in.

"Indeed," the Coyote Pirate said as he stood up.

146

Evey heard a faint boom outside followed by a series of popping noises. "What was . . . that?" she asked. "Are those people . . . yelling?"

The Coyote Pirate opened the lighthouse door. "Forgive me," he said while looking back at Evey. "Time truly is of the essence. I must try to stop them. Good luck to you—to us both."

Stop who? What does he mean? Evey thought. She tried to speak before the Coyote Pirate moved outside, but her jaw froze. She followed him out of the lighthouse, but her legs went numb and she collapsed. As she watched him disappear in the grass, the sound of people screaming grew louder. Evey closed her eyes. *Wake up!*

Whack! Evey sat up in her bed and banged her head on the top bunk. *I'm getting really tired of bunk beds!* she thought. She rubbed her sweaty forehead and took several deep breaths. Once her eyes adjusted, she scanned the room, then turned to the window. Hints of purple and pink from the coming sunrise replaced the moonlit sky. The crystal, still in her hand, had returned to its dull color.

Another vision—or memory—what does it mean? Evey thought. She bit her lip. *The sooner I find this lighthouse, the better, because I don't think I can take much more of this. I just hope I can convince my parents to let me come back.*

CHAPTER 19

The next day, Evey's parents, aunt, uncle, and Alex all arrived at Grandpa's for the Fourth of July weekend. After unpacking, the whole family drove to the Pancake Harbor Beach for an afternoon picnic. Evey invited Archer and his parents, so they planned on meeting them there.

Evey tried to stay upbeat during the drive, but she could not stop thinking about her parents' wishy-washy response to her asking to come back to Grandpa's in a few weeks.

I don't care about speech camp! Evey thought as she stared out the window at a farm. Dozens of grazing cows dotted the landscape. *It's not my fault you paid for camp already. I never wanted to go in the first place. A million speech therapy visits didn't stop me from embarrassing them by ordering boogers instead of burgers, so why do they think this will help? And why do I have to be home for Mom's friend's kid's birthday party? I never even see them.*

Evey tried to think of a different strategy. *I already told them about everything we've found and how historically important it is,* she thought. *I thought my parents were supposed to care about that type of stuff.*

Evey looked at a cherry orchard passing by the window. She saw hundreds of trees planted in neat lines, all covered in the little, red fruit. *Maybe if I focus on doing this for Grandma, they'll understand.* She took a moment to put her question together.

"Uh . . ." Evey mumbled.

"Yes, Evey?" her mom said.

"About coming back dear—I mean . . ."

"Remember your exercises. Think it out."

Evey ground her teeth. *Stop it already!* she thought. *I don't need you to tell me when I sound stupid!* She took a deep breath. "Grandma," she said. "This seemed . . . important to Grandma."

"Evey, we already talked about this," her mom said.

"But I tink see—no, I . . . think—"

"Evey," her dad cut in, "our answer isn't changing. I doubt we can do it. Besides, I think you've had enough time to do your research. Grandma didn't give you the crystal for it to become a chore. It was just a gift."

I've had enough time already! Evey thought. *Sorry I'm not smart enough to figure this out quicker. Maybe I should just sail to the island today and punch Finn in the face! Of course, then you'll still be mad at me and I'll just end up—*

"We're here!" Evey's dad said. She took a few deep breaths and rubbed her jaw. *Don't be so angry,* she thought. *It just makes me sound dumber.*

"You sure can tell the Fourth of July is tomorrow," Evey's dad said.

As they pulled into the parking lot, Evey noticed the usually quiet park was busy with the holiday crowd. A group of little kids ran around the playground. Teenagers played volleyball on both of the sand courts. Evey guessed over a

149

hundred people crowded the long, skinny beach. Dozens more swam in the water.

Evey's dad parked their car. The three of them unpacked their bags and a cooler from the trunk, then headed for the sand. Grandpa and Alex had already picked out a shady spot under a large tree. Evey and her mom lugged the cooler there and dropped it off. Archer and his parents met them shortly after.

Alex quickly smeared on sunscreen. "Can we go now?" he asked his mom.

"You might want to rub that in a little more," she said.

Evey looked at Alex as she applied her own sunscreen. Had she not been annoyed with her parents, she would have burst out laughing at the white streaks covering his face.

"Let's go!" Alex said after he hastily rubbed his face, arms, and legs.

Evey and Archer followed Alex to the long concrete pier that ran along the edge of the beach. Alex ran ahead to join the other kids jumping into the water. Evey updated Archer on her vision from the previous night.

"That's crazy," Archer said. "Are you sure you want to keep hanging on to that crystal? It's definitely messing with your brain."

Evey shrugged.

"If it makes you feel any better, I had a weird vision too," Archer said.

"Really?" Evey asked.

"Okay, it was probably just a dream, but it was still wild. I was playing in my school's badminton tournament. I destroyed my first few opponents, but in the championship match, I had to play against a coyote—but not a regular coyote. It was a robot, and it wore a pirate hat. It was impossible to beat. It used a sword instead of a racquet, and it kept howling at me. The dream ended with the coyote holding a trophy over me. I've been trying to figure out what it means. Maybe something about—"

Evey raised her eyebrow.

"Hurry up!" Alex yelled before Archer could respond. Evey waved at Alex to go ahead. He nodded and turned to the water. He jumped off the pier and tucked his legs into a cannonball, making a huge splash. After a few seconds, he popped back up shivering. "Come on! The water is only slightly freezing today!"

Archer turned back to Evey. "So, what do you think your vision means?" he asked.

"I don't know if it . . . matters . . ." Evey's voice trailed off.

"Why not?"

Evey looked over the edge of the pier as Alex started climbing up the ladder. The water was about five feet below her feet. She had jumped in every year since she could swim, but this year it reminded her of being thrown off the cliff. The memory gave her goosebumps.

"Evey?" Archer asked. "Did you hear me?"

"Uh . . . never mind," she said.

Alex ran by for another jump. "Let's go, slowpokes!" he yelled as he blasted off the pier.

Archer nudged Evey's shoulder. "Are we going?"

Evey nodded. She closed her eyes, took a deep breath, and jumped. She plugged her nose and straightened her body, then splashed into the cold water. Her skin shivering and tingling, she swam down until she touched the sandy bottom. She planted her feet, pushed off, and shot to the surface.

Archer jumped in next, making a big splash with a cannonball. He surfaced and shook his head, then swam toward Evey. "Did you talk to your parents about coming back in a few weeks?" he asked.

Ugh! Why did he have to bring it up? she thought. She kept quiet.

"Evey? Did you ask about our plan?"

Evey ground her teeth. "Not . . . not good," she mumbled.

Archer frowned as he reached the ladder. He pulled himself out of the water and started climbing. Evey followed. Alex jumped over them with another cannonball. Evey and Archer reached the top of the pier and moved away from the other kids so they could hear over the splashing. Evey rubbed her jaw, then told Archer what her parents said.

"That could still work out," Archer said. "It sounds like you might be able to come back if the timing is right."

Evey sighed. "Archer, I have like tree days—I mean . . . three days my parents . . . will let me come back. I doubt . . . that's going to be the . . . right time. And I need . . . somebody to . . . drive me here."

Archer shrugged. "Sorry, I'm just trying to be positive."

Being positive can be annoying, Evey thought. She bit her lip to stop from saying anything rude. "I don't . . . think it was a good . . . plan," she said instead. "Even if . . . Finn's gone, the other . . . East Siders . . . might be . . . there."

"I guess," Archer said.

"Maybe . . . we can go . . . tomorrow. The East Siders . . . might be distracted by . . . the fireworks."

Archer scratched his neck. "I don't know, Evey. I like to think of myself as brave and all, but there's like six of them. Fighting a bunch of obnoxious kids is not my idea of a fun Fourth of July. Maybe we should just wait."

"Until den!" Evey shouted. She rubbed her jaw and looked at Archer. *You know what I mean*, she thought.

"You don't have to yell at me," Archer said.

Evey felt her face turn red. Her Triforce burned. *Stupid moles!* she thought. She glared at Archer. *You obviously don't care about this as much as I do! You just act like you're in some stupid movie! Maybe that's because you can talk normal and you don't have to worry about anything!*

"If you're just going to stare at me like you want to punch me, I'm going to leave," Archer said. He started walking away.

"Tarry!" Evey blurted out. She rubbed her eyes. Archer stopped and turned around. "Sorry," she repeated. "I'm mad, but I don't . . . want to it you—I mean . . . hit. I just . . . need to . . . find the . . . light . . . house! This is . . . pressurc! I can't . . . handle it. I'm . . . seeing my grandma's . . . memories. I'm . . . talking to a dead pirate. None of it makes right—I mean, it doesn't make dense—no, it . . . ugh!"

"Doesn't make sense," Archer said quietly.

Evey nodded as she rubbed her temples.

"Do you think maybe it's time to get our parents involved?" Archer asked.

"No!" Evey said. "If I tell them about the . . . visions . . . they'll . . . think I'm crazy . . . or they'll . . . take the crystal. And tin I ask tem to elp, tay make me deal . . ." Evey stopped talking and grunted.

"You don't have to say anything else," Archer said. "I know this is really important to you. But look at it this way—if the key to this big secret is hidden under the lighthouse on Coyote Island, it's been there for over a hundred and fifty years. I don't think it's going anywhere."

"Come on slowpokes!" Alex yelled as he ran by for another jump.

Archer watched Alex blast off the pier. "Evey, I don't think you're in the mood for jokes," he said, "but I can't resist. We should just send Alex to the island. I don't think he'd mind if the East Siders threw him off the cliff."

Evey cracked a small smile. "Maybe . . . you're right," she said. "It isn't worth a . . . a fight."

"The East Siders can't be there forever, right? In the meantime, let's just enjoy the Fourth. Eat way too much food, hit up the parade, eat way too much candy, and fireworks!"

Evey nodded, then paused. "I almost . . . forgot," she said. "The . . . Championship."

"What?" Archer asked.

"My family—mainly my grandpa, dad, and uncle—we all . . . face off in a bunch of games. Whoever . . . wins the most . . . points gets . . . the turtle hat."

"Turtle hat?" Archer asked. "This conversation took a weird turn. And that's saying something since we were just talking about a dead pirate."

"It's like . . . like a . . . championship belt."

"Oh, I get it. I want a championship turtle hat. Can I play? I bet I'd win if you included badminton. Jeez, I love badminton. Anyway, your family is cool. Still weird too, but cool weird. Not like my family. My family is just weird-weird. You know what I mean?"

Evey shrugged.

Alex, exhausted and dripping wet, ran over to Evey and Archer. "What's with you two?" he asked in between deep breaths. "Are you going to jump or talk about your silly, dead pirate all day?"

Archer stuck out his hands. "Let's all go on the count of three. It will be the biggest cannonball ever!" The three grabbed hands and lined up side-by-side. "One, two, three!" They jumped off the pier and crashed into the water, making a giant splash.

Evey, Archer, and Alex jumped a few more times, then walked to the beach for dinner. Evey felt her stomach rumble once she saw the food spread on the picnic table. The buffet included her dad's guacamole and chips, her aunt's pasta salad, and Grandpa's stuffed peppers. Archer's parents brought a giant bowl of fruit, as well as cheese and crackers. Evey, Archer, and Alex took turns filling their plates, then excitedly dug into their food.

After eating, Evey, Archer, and Alex tossed a football with Evey's dad and uncle.

"Dad, are you ready for the Championship?" Alex asked.

"Going for the three-peat!" he replied.

Evey's dad looked at her and shook his head. He mouthed "He's going down." Evey laughed.

Evey's uncle looked over. "Wait and see. We start tonight!"

Evey chimed in. "Grandpa's been . . . practicing. He took me mini . . . golfing a lot. And he made me play . . . foosball and . . . ping-pong."

155

"He hasn't won the Championship in years," Evey's uncle said. "He's no threat. Especially in mini-golf."

Evey noticed her dad laughing to himself. "Remember when Grandpa fell in the pond at Pirate Park," he said.

Evey's uncle laughed. "That was hilarious!"

Evey and Alex looked at each other confused. "We never heard this one," Alex said.

Evey's dad tossed the ball. "Grandpa was having a great round of mini-golf. He was ahead by like six strokes halfway through, but then he started slipping. He still had a small lead on the last hole—the one with the pirate ship that swings back-and-forth. It stopped his ball three or four times, causing him to lose the round. He was stomping around so mad that he stumbled over some rocks and fell into a pond. It was great!"

Is that what that picture in the photo album was—the one Grandpa skipped past? Evey wondered.

Archer turned to Evey. "Are they always like this?" he asked.

Evey rolled her eyes.

"Don't pay attention to her," Alex said. "She's just jealous because last year she didn't win any points. Just a big zero."

Evey stuck her tongue out at Alex. "All you care about is that . . . the Championship ends at . . . Chester's."

Alex's eyes lit up. "That's right! Blue Moon here I come!"

"Blue Moon?" Archer asked.

Evey put her finger in her mouth as if to gag herself.

"Don't listen to Ms. Vanilla over there," Alex said.

Evey turned to Archer. "Mini-golf and Chester's . . . will be the day after the . . . Fourth. Want to come?"

"Count me in!" Archer said.

CHAPTER 20

Evey and Alex ran out Grandpa's front door and headed to the garage. "Do we have enough time to get to the parade?" Alex asked. "I don't want to miss the candy."

"We'll be . . . fine," Evey said as they reached the garage. They stopped when they saw Grandpa and Evey's uncle playing the final ping-pong match in round three of the Championship.

"Whoa," Alex said. "This looks close. Let's watch."

Alex is right, Evey thought. She could tell from the nervous, sweaty faces on Grandpa and her uncle. She walked to the side of the ping-pong table where her parents watched from two stools. "Score?" she asked.

"Grandpa is losing by one," Evey's mom said.

Grandpa scored a point and pumped his fist.

"All tied up now," Evey's dad said. "Next point wins!"

The Championship started the night before. Evey's uncle took the early lead by winning the first round—a four-hour family game of Risk. Round two took place first thing on the morning of the Fourth. The family took the pontoon boat out to fish. Evey and her parents came up empty. Alex and his mom each caught a small perch, earning them both a point.

Grandpa and Evey's uncle each caught a bass, but Grandpa's was bigger, giving him the win.

Looking to take the lead with ping-pong, Grandpa prepared to serve. Evey could tell from the way he held the ball that he planned to use his spin serve. He twirled the ball between his thumb and index finger as he stared at Evey's uncle.

"Hurry up, old man!" Evey's uncle said.

Grandpa glared at him, then turned his focus back to the ball. He gently tossed it in the air and hit it with a sweeping motion of the paddle. Evey watched the ball fly over the net and curve toward the edge of the table. Grandpa hit a perfect spin serve, but her uncle was ready. He quickly moved to his side and returned the serve. Evey thought the two volleyed back-and-forth for what felt like ten minutes. Her uncle slowly worked the ball toward the edge of the table to make Grandpa stretch. He hit a perfect shot, nearly out of Grandpa's reach. Grandpa lunged and managed to hit the ball back over the net, but it lofted high in the air. Evey's uncle waited patiently for the ball to hit the table, then he smashed it. Grandpa tried to swing at the ball, but whiffed. It bounced off his side of the table and flew into the driveway.

"No!" Grandpa shouted. "I was so close!"

"Nice!" Alex said. He ran over and gave his dad a high-five.

Evey's dad looked at Grandpa. "Second place again," he said. "You're turning into the Buffalo Bills."

Evey raised her eyebrow.

"It's a nineties football thing," her mom said.

I guess there's no end to these references, Evey thought. She turned to the bikes. "Come on, Alex, we . . . have to meet Archer," she said. The two grabbed bikes and helmets from the garage and pedaled down the driveway, then turned up the road toward Archer's house.

"Do you know the score?" Alex asked.

Evey ran the numbers in her head. Her family used an excessively complicated scoring system in the Championship. "Your dad . . . thirteen, Grandpa—eight, and my dad . . . four."

"And only foosball and mini-golf are left," Alex said. "Ha! My dad's going to get the three-peat."

Archer waited on his bike at the end of his driveway. "What took you two so long?" he said as Evey and Archer approached.

"Sorry, fishing and ping-pong," Evey said.

"No worries," Archer said. "I was schooling my mom in badminton. Did you catch any fish?"

Alex chuckled.

"Sounds like you cleaned out the lake," Archer said with a smile.

"Evey caught a tadpole!" Alex said.

Evey rolled her eyes and sped up to ride in front. Once the three reached the end of the street, they turned onto the Turtle Lake bridge. Evey found it difficult to not think about her grandma's crystal and the lighthouse when she saw Coyote Island in the distance. She had brought her notes and maps in her backpack in case she decided to observe the island on the way back.

Let it go, Evey thought as she turned her gaze back to the bridge. *Remember, I just want to have fun today.*

Once the three passed the bridge, they took a backroad into town as the highway was already closed for the parade.

They pedaled to the town park near the marina and set their bikes and helmets down. Alex ran ahead to a spot on the side of the road just as the parade started a little south of them.

"It started!" Alex said as Evey and Archer joined him on the sidewalk.

Evey peered down the road. A large, red fire truck led the parade. She could hear alternating sounds of horns, sirens, and the high school band. When the fire truck approached, she joined the crowd in cheering as it blared its siren again. Behind the fire truck, a parade of cars and floats from local businesses followed.

"There it is!" Alex said when he spotted the Sweet Shop's car. He pulled a bag from his pocket and opened it up. Evey and Archer did the same. Every year, the Sweet Shop staff drove an old, pink convertible. Evey, Archer, and Alex waved as the car drove by and threw handfuls of homemade candy. Alex and Archer stuffed their bags with everything in sight. Evey targeted the vanilla fudge pretzels.

The high school band approached next. Evey recognized their song as the theme from *Star Wars*. Archer found a stick and waved it at Evey like a lightsaber. Evey responded by pretending to use the force to choke him. He played along, dropping his stick and falling to the ground.

"It figures you two would like *Star Wars*," Alex said.

"You have a problem with the force?" Archer responded.

"*Star Trek* is a thousand times more realistic, and a million times better. But *Star Wars* makes sense given the pirate ghost nonsense you two were talking about at the beach."

Archer pointed the stick at Alex. "You sound like Anakin whining about not being a Jedi Master," he said.

161

Alex crossed his arms. "Anakin is lame and those movies stink. How do you . . ."

Evey rolled her eyes and turned back to the parade. After a few minutes, her favorite float approached. It was an antique truck painted red, white, and blue. Historical American flags with different numbers of stars covered the truck.

"Look!" Archer shouted. "It's Professor Paulsen! Hi Professor!"

Evey was so distracted by the flags that she did not notice Professor Paulsen riding in the front seat. A banner on the side of the truck read "Door County Historical Museum."

I never knew the museum sponsors this truck, Evey thought while looking at the flags. She waved excitedly. Professor Paulsen waved back and prompted the driver to honk the truck's horn. After it passed by, the three kids made a final sweep for candy, then walked to their bikes.

"What time is it?" Archer asked.

"Eleven," Evey said. "We have an . . . hour until . . ." her voice trailed off.

"Something wrong?"

Evey pointed down the street. Finn and three of his friends sat on a bench eating candy.

"East Siders," Archer said in his deep, dramatic voice.

Alex looked up from his bag of candy. "Those are the kids you've been talking about?"

Evey nodded.

"They don't look tough," Alex said. "You should just fight them for control of that island."

"You're more than welcome to go ahead and try," Archer said.

"Whatever," Alex said. "Let's go to the peninsula to eat our candy."

Evey and Archer agreed. The three mounted their bikes and pedaled away from the East Siders. They rode down the street until they reached the entrance to the peninsula—a long, skinny trail that extended into the bay.

Large boulders lined each side of the trail. Evey, Archer, and Alex pedaled down the path to the far tip of the peninsula. After setting their bikes down, they walked to a bench overlooking the water and sat down.

"Yikes, a little windy out here!" Archer said as he held on to his Bears hat. He almost needed to yell for everybody to hear him.

Waves from the bay hit the rocks around the bench with enough force to occasionally splash them. Evey tightened her grip on her bag of candy to stop it from blowing away.

"Whoa, parasailers!" Alex said.

Evey and Archer looked at the water. A speedboat zipped by. A long cable ran from the back of the boat high into the air. The cable attached to a harness holding two riders, their feet dangling freely in the air. A big, blue parachute trailed above and behind them.

"Talk about a great way to see the parade," Archer said. "Have either of you ever gone parasailing?"

Evey and Alex shook their heads no.

"I went with my sisters once," Archer said. "You could see for miles. We were really high in the air. It was cool—totally terrifying—but still cool. Scary cool. Jeez, when I really think about it . . ."

Evey zoned out and stared at the waves while Archer continued his story. *Maybe we should just go to the island now,* she thought. *Most of the East Siders are here. No, Archer's right. We could be there for hours searching, and they'd eventually spot our boat. The last thing I need is to get thrown off the cliff or covered in paintballs again. Besides, I do need a break. Hopefully, tonight we can just watch fireworks and relax.*

Evey rubbed her temples. *And maybe figure out a way to get a point in the Championship,* she thought. *I really don't want to deal with Alex making fun of me for another year. Speaking of which, why can't I ever catch a fish?* Evey looked at her grandma's crystal, dangling from her neck. *I guess the Coyote Pirate can—*

The sound of laughter from behind the bench snapped Evey out of her daze. She turned around and froze.

"What's wrong?" Archer asked.

Down the path and next to their bikes, Evey saw Finn digging in her backpack. Three other East Siders huddled around him.

"Hey!" Archer yelled.

Finn took a notebook and map out of Evey's backpack. "Let's go!" he yelled.

No! Evey thought. She and Archer jumped off the bench and ran to their bikes. Alex, juggling his bag of candy, trailed behind.

Finn and the other East Siders grabbed their own bikes and rode up the peninsula toward the road. Evey jumped on her bike and pushed the pedals, but she heard a grinding noise. She looked down and saw her chain tangled up.

"Mine too," Archer said. "Punks."

Evey threw her bike to the ground. She clenched her fists as she watched Finn stop by the street and look back. He smiled and waved, then rode out of sight.

"What was in there?" Alex asked.

"Everting!" Evey shouted. Her jaw tightened and her eyes watered. *Why did I leave my backpack there!* she thought. *What is wrong with me! It's bad enough I can't find the lighthouse, but now Finn is going to find it! Why do I always have to screw up!*

Alex looked through Evey's backpack. "You mean your stuff on the Pirate and the crystal?" he said.

Evey ignored Alex as she tried to hold back her tears. Archer looked at him and nodded, then turned back to Evey. "Come on, Evey, we should go find our parents."

CHAPTER 21

Evey, Archer, and Alex took a few minutes to fix the chains on their bikes, then pedaled to the Fourth of July festival at the town park. Hundreds of people in the park's front lawn rummaged through tent-covered booths selling garden decorations, clothes, and desserts. On the other side of the park, a band blasted the type of classic rock music that Grandpa listened to. Evey's nose told her the food tents were grilling barbeque pork and corn.

Alex spotted their families on the outskirts of the booths. The three set their bikes against a nearby tree and walked toward them. Evey saw her parents in a photography booth. She kept her head down and moved slowly, fearing they would notice her watery eyes.

"Something wrong, Evey?" her mom asked.

Seriously, how does she do that? Evey thought. She kept her head down.

Evey's mom walked over and put her hands on Evey's shoulders. "Evey, what's the matter?" she asked.

Stop asking me! Evey thought. *You already said I've had enough time to figure this mystery out, so there's no point telling you!*

Evey's dad pulled away from a large picture of a cave. "What's going on?" he asked.

Evey started crying. *Just leave me alone!* she thought.

"What is it?" her parents said at the same time.

Evey covered her eyes and sobbed. Her mom wrapped an arm around her and led her to an open spot in the grass. Evey sat down and pulled her knees to her chest. Her mom rubbed her back. "Try to calm down," her mom said. "Take some deep breaths."

Evey's dad kneeled down on the grass next to her. "Whatever it is, I'm sure it'll be fine," he said.

It'll be fine? Evey thought as she continued sobbing. *Then why should I bother talking to you?*

"Evey, try to tell us," her mom said.

"I don't . . . I . . . I—" Evey closed her mouth and grunted. *Even if I did want to talk to you, I can't even say the words!* she thought.

"Put your thoughts together," her dad said.

"I'm tying!" Evey shouted. She rubbed her temples.

"Okay . . . we just, uh . . ." her dad mumbled.

Her mom jumped in. "We're just trying to see what's wrong so we can help."

"I don't daunt door elp!" Evey snapped.

"Evey, we see you're upset," her dad said, "but you don't need to shout at us."

Evey brushed her mom's arm away, stood up, and stormed out of the park and crossed the street to the marina. She walked halfway down the pier and took a seat on one of the benches overlooking the water.

Evey took a deep breath as she stared at the waves rolling into the bay. The strong breeze coming from the lake felt good on her hot face. She stopped crying and wiped the tears from her eyes.

My parents never want to help, Evey thought. *Unless you count pointing out every time I screw up! If I tell them about Finn, they'll just be more disappointed in me. I guess they're right, though. Grandma gave me her crystal to figure out this mystery, and I failed. What else is new? I can't talk good enough, my grades aren't good enough, and I'm never—*

"Can I sit down, Evey?"

Evey flinched and turned around. Grandpa stood a few feet from the bench. Evey nodded at him, then turned back to the water. Grandpa took a seat next to her and stretched out his legs. He sat quietly for several minutes. Evey looked to her side and saw his eyes closed.

"Are you . . . napping?" Evey whispered.

"What, no?" Grandpa said as he popped upright and opened his eyes. "Sorry. It's hot and I just ate a lot. That combo always wipes me out."

Evey rolled her eyes.

"I wanted to check on you," Grandpa said, "but you found too relaxing of a spot—just like your grandma."

Evey shrugged.

"Did I ever tell you about our old boat?" Grandpa asked.

"The . . . sailboat?" Evey responded.

"No, I mean *Tank*."

Evey raised her eyebrow.

"I'm talking about our first boat, before the pontoon." A big smile spread across Grandpa's face. "Boy, did I love *Tank*. It was more of a lake cruiser. It was twenty feet long, and it had a nice cabin with a bathroom, kitchen, and bed. And a big area out back to sit or fish."

"Why did you . . . name . . . *Tank*?" Evey asked.

"It was made of aluminum, which is much stronger than the fiberglass used on most boats. Plus, it was a beautiful silver color. People always thought it was a Coast Guard boat."

Evey turned her body toward Grandpa to listen more closely.

"Your grandma and I liked taking it out," he said, "but a lot of the time we would just relax at the marina."

"Why . . . you keep it . . . here?" Evey asked.

"That was before we had the Turtle Lake house. Back then, we owned a tiny cottage that wasn't by the water. We wanted something bigger, so we sold *Tank*."

Evey raised her eyebrow.

"It was an expensive boat," Grandpa said. "We were able to use the money from selling it to buy the pontoon and put the down payment on the Turtle Lake house. It took some time for your grandma to convince me, but she was right. The new house and the pontoon hold a lot more people, so they're better for the family."

Evey frowned. *I wish my parents acted that nice,* she thought.

"Evey," Grandpa continued, "I brought your grandma up because you should know that she fought with your dad a lot back in the day. We both did, actually, but Grandma especially."

"Why?"

"Oh, you know—family stuff. We all do things that rub each other the wrong way."

Evey nodded. *Like my parents pointing out every word I say wrong,* she thought.

169

"Speaking of which," Grandpa said, "do you want to tell me what happened back there? Alex told me about the kids you ran into at the peninsula, but it looked like you were more upset with your parents."

Evey's jaw tightened. "I . . . don't . . . I . . ." her voice trailed off.

"I don't care if you mess up your words, Evey. Just shout it out if you need to. It'll help."

Evey took a deep breath. "My parents . . . make me . . . they just . . ." She took another deep breath. "They don't . . . help."

"Evey, I'm sure they'll help if—"

"No!" Evey shouted. She wiped away tears from her cheeks. "Tarry," she mumbled.

Grandpa put an arm around Evey's shoulder. "You never have to be sorry for how you feel," he said.

Evey started weeping again, and words poured out of her before she could process them. "Why do my parents act ike I'n am idiot! I tie ard to alk right, but dare mever appy! Tay point out ever mitake! Keep pacticing! More ezzercises! Another peach camp!" Evey's voice grew louder until she shouted. "I used to ack for elp, but ever time tay nade me eel ike a dailure!"

Evey buried her face in Grandpa's shoulder and sobbed. Grandpa held her until her tears stopped. After a few minutes, she pulled away, wiped her face, and turned toward the lake.

"Evey," Grandpa said, "your parents—all of us—we do want to help you."

"Ten hi do you lad at me?" Evey snapped, causing Grandpa to recoil. "Laugh," she carefully corrected. "Booger . . . instead of . . . burger."

Grandpa started to speak, but stopped himself.

Told you, Evey thought.

"I'm sorry about that," Grandpa said. "I didn't mean to hurt your feelings. It's just—I think I'm so used to the way you talk that I don't look at things like that as a mistake. Sometimes, it's just funny. Like this one time after I beat your dad and uncle in a game of Risk, I meant to tell them how much smarter I am, but instead I said, 'I'm farter.'"

Evey chuckled, then shook her head. "But I do it all . . . always."

"True," Grandpa said, "but there's more to you than how you talk. You're a great runner for starters."

"I run because I tink at other ports," Evey said. "And I'm one of the lowest—" she stopped herself, grunted loudly, and rubbed her temples. "Slowest," she said.

"You're also very smart."

"Not my . . . my grades."

"You're great with maps," Grandpa wearily said.

Evey rolled her eyes.

Grandpa sighed. "You're right, Evey. I'm not helping. It's just instinct to try to say positive things when you're upset." Grandpa leaned back on the bench and rubbed his chin for a moment. "How about instead I tell you more about those fights I mentioned?"

Evey nodded.

"After high school, your dad got into a fancy college and entered their pre-law program. Your grandma and I were so proud of him. But, after a year, he dropped out."

Evey raised both her eyebrows.

Grandpa rubbed his chin again. "He never told you that?"

Evey shook her head no.

"Oh," Grandpa said. "In that case, don't tell him I told you. I think he's still embarrassed about it, even though he shouldn't be."

"But he went to . . . college," Evey said. "He . . . he loves . . . ISU."

"He did, and he did great there. But that was after he left the other school and took a year off. Eventually, your grandma and I realized your dad was just struggling to figure out what he wanted to do with his life. But when he dropped out, we thought he couldn't handle the work. Grandma was devastated. She did everything to try to convince your dad to change his mind. When he didn't, she couldn't hide her disappointment. That drove your dad nuts. He accused us of not supporting him, we lost our cool, and the three of us argued for hours. It took a long time to patch things up. The whole thing was . . . unfortunate."

Evey watched a tear roll down Grandpa's cheek.

"It was unfortunate because it didn't have to happen," Grandpa continued. "Your dad thought we were disappointed in him. But really, we were disappointed in *ourselves*. We thought we failed to prepare him. We were afraid we . . . ruined his life."

Evey squinted as she thought about Grandpa's story. "But if you and Grandma . . . felt that way, hi not—I mean . . . why not tell him—my dad?"

"A lot of times, I think people aren't fully aware of feelings like that. I know we weren't—not at the time. It's like our brains look for ways to pass the blame somewhere else, without us even recognizing it. It's probably the same reason why I keep making excuses about losing the Championship." Grandpa straightened his glasses. "My brain doesn't want to admit your dad or uncle are better."

Evey briefly smiled.

"But seriously," Grandpa continued, "Grandma and I felt like we failed your dad. He felt like he failed too. But none of us could fully understand, let alone deal with, the anger and sadness that created. So, we ended up turning those feelings on each other. I don't think anybody did it on purpose. It just happens sometimes."

"How did that . . . fight end?" Evey asked.

"It just took some time for everybody to calm down and communicate more clearly. And remember my story about *Tank*?"

Evey nodded.

"I know we hurt your dad's feelings, but in the end, he realized that a lot of what your grandma did—like selling our old boat—was because she loved her family so much."

Evey rubbed her temples as she thought about Grandpa's story. "Why . . . tell me diss . . . this?"

Grandpa leaned closer to Evey. "Because I see a lot of similarities between that story and what's going on with you and your parents."

Evey looked at the water and squinted again. *Is he saying my parents are disappointed in themselves—not me?* she wondered. *But that doesn't explain why they jump all over my speech mistakes—or does it?* Evey turned to Grandpa. "My parents . . . think they're . . . failing me?" she asked.

Grandpa nodded.

"So," Evey continued, "they try to . . . help me, to . . . feel better, or . . . feel like . . ."

"Like they're good parents," Grandpa finished.

Evey shook her head. "But tay get so trust—I mean . . . frustrated . . . with me. Why?"

"Why were you so frustrated back in the park? Did your parents say anything mean to you?"

"Yes . . ." Evey stopped herself. *They tried to get me to tell them why I was crying. I guess that's not mean. Definitely annoying—like really annoying—but not mean. So, why am I so mad?*

"Let me rephrase that question," Grandpa said. "Why does the Door County Pirate mystery matter so much to you?"

Evey felt more tears flood her eyes. She bit her lip and looked down. *Because I thought it would make my parents proud of me,* she thought. *Make them see something other than my speech disorder.*

"Evey?" Grandpa said.

Evey took a deep breath. "I taught I . . . could . . ." her voice cracked, ". . . parents . . . proud."

"You thought solving this would make them proud?"

Evey nodded.

"That makes sense," Grandpa said. "And when those kids stole your stuff, how did it make you feel?"

Evey wiped a few tears from her cheeks. "Like a . . . failure," she said.

Grandpa nodded. "That's a hard feeling to deal with, Evey. That type of anger hurts. I know from experience. It's easy to turn that on somebody else, like—"

"My parents," Evey cut in.

Grandpa nodded.

Evey shrugged. "It's . . . hard not to get . . . mad at . . . them. I . . . feel like . . . they're mever around to . . . see good . . . stuff I do, but they're always dare to tell me when I ness—or . . . mess up."

"I can see how that's irritating," Grandpa said. "And honestly, you probably need to tell them that sometime. But you should try to see their perspective too. Remember, it took you way longer to start talking than most kids. And once a doctor labeled you with a speech disorder, your parents were afraid they'd never be able to understand you. So, they invested so much time and energy in helping you overcome it. And it worked. Sure, you jumble stuff up sometimes and you pause, but we understand you. And believe me, your parents are proud of how hard you've worked."

Evey closed her eyes. *I hope you're right,* she thought.

"Did you catch all of that, Evey?" Grandpa asked.

Evey opened her eyes. She slowly nodded. "But they . . . still act . . . annoying."

Grandpa smirked. "Evey, they're family," he said. "Haven't you ever heard that saying—'Friends welcome, family by appointment?'"

Evey laughed. *I need a sign with that saying in my room,* she thought. "I guess I need to be . . . nicer," she said.

"Don't beat yourself up. Right now, I'm sure your parents are doing the same thing as you—going from being angry to feeling guilty about how they handled things. Especially your dad."

Evey raised her eyebrow.

"You know, Evey," Grandpa said, "you and your dad are very similar in a lot of ways. It's not just that eyebrow and your boring taste in desserts."

Evey rolled her eyes. *Seriously, what do people have against vanilla ice cream?* she thought.

"What I mean is," Grandpa continued, "when he was young, he used to say he wanted to do something that mattered. It's like he was trying to prove to the world he was good enough."

Evey put her head in her hands. *Like I want to I prove that I'm not just a girl who can't talk.*

Grandpa rubbed Evey's back. "You okay?" he asked.

Evey took a deep breath. "Just tinking," she said.

"And?"

Evey looked at Grandpa. "I want to . . . prove . . . I'm more than . . . speech disorder. I guess that's . . . dumb."

"It's not dumb. There's nothing wrong with feeling self-conscious about your speech."

Evey raised her eyebrow again.

"I know everybody always says not to feel that way," Grandpa said. "But the truth is, you can't pretend those feelings are not there. Even if you solve this pirate mystery and start speaking perfectly, your brain would just find something else to feel insecure about. In that way, you're just like everybody else."

"Then . . . what are you . . . in . . . secure about?" Evey asked.

"Not much, honestly. Not caring about things is one of the perks of getting old."

Evey laughed. "Serious," she said.

Grandpa crossed his arms. "Well, for a long time, I was really self-conscious about my gray spot."

The gray spot? Evey thought.

Grandpa turned so Evey could see the back of his head. "See that little thing?" he said. "I've had that since I was a kid. People made fun of me for it. I hated it for the longest time, but eventually I realized it kind of made me unique. And now that everybody my age is all gray, it makes me look younger."

"I taught you dyed your—" Evey covered her mouth before she finished the sentence. She looked at Grandpa. He frowned, but then burst out laughing. Evey did the same. After quieting down, Evey asked, "How do you mow—I mean . . . know . . . all . . . this?"

"I've read a few psychology books," Grandpa said.

Evey raised both eyebrows.

Grandpa laughed again. "Why do you think I sleep so late—I'm always reading at night! I have to keep my mind sharp to stay ahead of your dad and uncle in some ways. Speaking of that, your dad beat me in foosball earlier, but I still won some points for the Championship. I'm only two behind your uncle for the overall lead. We need to get serious about mini-golf tomorrow. I need to win, and if you could beat your uncle too, to drive him down in the standings, that would help."

Evey bit her lip. "Grandpa, he's . . . good."

"I know, but you did great our last round."

"That . . . was practice—not a game. Besides, my dad could . . . still win too."

Grandpa leaned back on the bench. "That might be even worse. Whenever your dad beats me, I have to listen to him ask if I 'smell what the Rock is cooking.'"

Evey laughed. "Why does he . . . say that?"

"It's some silly thing a wrestler said in the nineties. And I think that's where he got that eyebrow too."

Evey turned back to the lake. She saw a few gulls dive in and out of the choppy water. A fishing boat bobbed up and down in the distance. She took her grandma's crystal out from under her shirt and held it up to see it sparkle in the sunlight.

It's okay to feel insecure, because everybody else does too, she told herself. *I don't know if that applies to Archer. I feel like nothing bothers him—except maybe silence. I wonder about Finn, though. What's he insecure about? He did act a little—*

Grandpa cleared his throat. "Evey?"

Evey turned back to him. "I'm just . . . thinking. This . . . helps with . . . my parents, but not . . . with the light . . . house."

"Evey, do you still think you need to solve this mystery to make your parents proud?"

Evey shook her head no.

"Then, why do you still want to?" Grandpa asked.

Evey closed her eyes. She thought about Archer's funny rambling. She remembered sailing the *Sunrise* to Blueberry Island. She imagined the museum's maps that she studied. A large smile spread across Evey's face. She opened her eyes and looked at Grandpa. "It's been . . . fun."

Grandpa grinned. "In that case, tell me what you need to beat those kids to the lighthouse."

Evey started to raise her eyebrow, but stopped. "I like the . . . sound of that," she said.

CHAPTER 22

Evey and Grandpa walked back to the park. With the band taking a break, Evey thought that the area sounded unusually quiet. She found her parents sitting on a large bale of hay near the stage.

Evey's dad held out a grilled corn cob for her. "We got you some corn, Evey," he said.

"Tanks," she said as she grabbed the corn and sat down. She took a few bites. Her family often ate corn on the cob during the summer, but they always boiled it. The smokey flavor from the grill made it more of a treat. Her parents knew she loved it.

After working through half of her corn, Evey opened her mouth, but nothing came out. *Why is this so hard?* she thought. She nibbled at her corn again while she tried to think of what to say.

Evey's dad slid closer to her. "I know talking about things that make you upset is hard for you, Evey. It is for me too." Her dad looked at all of the people surrounding them, then whispered, "And who wants to talk about this stuff with so many people around?"

Evey nodded in agreement. "I'm . . . sorry," she mumbled.

"We're sorry too, Evey," her mom said as she reached over her dad and held Evey's hand.

Let the record show that I said it first, Evey thought.

"Just know that whatever you're upset about," her mom continued, "we're confident you can deal with it. But if you need help, you can ask us any time."

Evey nodded. *Thank goodness,* she thought. *My brain is way too exhausted to talk about this now.* "I . . . will tell you . . . later," she said. "Right now, I'm . . . distracted."

Evey's dad jumped in. "We get it. We know you have a lot going on researching your crystal."

"You mean . . . Grandma's crystal?" Evey said.

"No, I mean *your* crystal. It's yours now, Evey. And remember, Grandma wanted you to have fun with it—have an adventure. And based on everything you told us about your pirate mystery, I think you're on the right track."

My crystal? Evey thought. She smiled as she repeated the words to herself. She leaned into her dad's chest. Her mom reached over and the three hugged.

Once the family pulled apart, Evey's dad stood up. "I need some more corn," he said. "Alex and Archer seemed worried about you. Why don't you check in with them?" Evey nodded just as the band started playing a guitar-heavy song. "Whoa, they're busting out a classic!" her dad said excitedly. He began air guitaring. "Flyyyy away . . . yea!" he crudely sang.

"Nineties song?" Evey asked her mom.

"Yes," her mom said with a squeamish face. "But your dad's definitely not doing it any justice."

Evey laughed with her mom as her dad continued singing, then walked over to a picnic table where Archer, Alex, and their parents sat. "Can we talk?" she asked. The two followed Evey to the playground, where they all took seats on the swings.

"Feeling any better?" Archer asked.

"Yea," Evey said as she started pumping her legs back and forth on the swing.

"Good, because I got Alex onboard with our mission to find the lighthouse."

Evey looked at Alex. "You'll . . . help?" she asked.

"Sure," Alex said. "I want you to get even with those kids."

"You . . . believe in all of . . . this?" Evey asked.

"Let's not go that far," Alex replied. "I don't think we're actually going to find anything out there, but it's the principle of the matter. And it's not like I have much else to do without my Legos."

"Super strong endorsement of the mission, Alex," Archer said. "Anyway, I was thinking the East Siders probably won't know what to do with your notes. Alex and I were talking about the next time we'll all be up here—"

"We can't wait," Evey said.

Archer brought his swing to a stop. "What do you mean?" he asked.

"I don't . . . think we can risk it. The East Siders probably know the land . . . island. And my notes and map make every . . . thing pretty clear. We have to assume they can . . . find the . . . lighthouse. And this isn't some . . . silly thing we're looking for. It's . . . important."

"Good point," Archer said. "The fate of the world probably does rest on whatever supernatural secret that lighthouse leads to."

Alex rolled his eyes. "Take it down a notch, Archer," he said. "Remember, even if we get on the island when the East Siders are not there, they'll probably show up before we find the lighthouse."

"Not that I want to do this," Archer said, "but maybe we could get our parents involved."

Alex shook his head. "Do you think anybody will believe us? Tell them we need help fending off these kids to find a supernatural secret—they'll think we're crazy or playing a prank."

Archer shrugged.

"Alex is right," Evey said. "But we can . . . do it alone."

"How?" Archer asked.

"I came up . . . with a plan. It's . . . risky, but Grandpa agreed to . . . help."

"You got Grandpa in on this?" Alex asked.

Evey smiled. "You know he likes it . . . when we . . . break rules."

"Very true."

"Risky?" Archer said. "Breaking the rules? Your grandpa? I don't know if I should be excited or scared."

"If you're both in," Evey said, "we should . . . leave . . . now."

Archer and Alex both looked confused. "Now?" they said together.

Evey nodded. "We're going to Coyote Island . . . tonight."

CHAPTER 23

The crowd clapped as the first firework exploded into a ball of orange lights. The sparks shot outward into the twilight sky, then slowly fell to the lake. Evey heard a collective sigh once everybody realized that the lone firework came from a resident on Turtle Lake instead the town. Apple Bay's professional show was not scheduled to begin until the last bit of light disappeared from the sky.

Local residents lined up along the Turtle Lake bridge to watch the event. While most of the crowd faced the town, Evey, Archer, and Alex sat on other side of the bridge, observing Coyote Island. Evey pulled a pair of binoculars from her backpack and peered through them. She tried to block out the music, the thump of bean bags hitting boards, and the constant chatter as she focused on her plan.

"Finn's boat is . . . there," Evey said. "But I only . . . see two East Siders."

"What are they doing?" Archer asked.

"I think . . . they're looking for us. The rest must be . . . searching for . . . the light . . . house." Evey put the binoculars down and bit her lip.

"What's the plan, Evey?" Alex asked. "We can't just sail up and dock if they're guarding the beach."

"We go to the . . . cliff," Evey said.

"What?" Alex said. "Since when is there a cliff in this plan?"

"It's a rock . . . wall covered in tree roots. We can climb it to avoid . . . the beach." Evey turned to Archer. "Besides, we need the cliff to . . . find the clearing," she said.

Archer and Alex both looked uneasy.

Evey raised her eyebrow.

Archer sighed. "It just sounds a little risky."

"It wouldn't be an . . . adventure . . . without risk," Evey said. "Isn't that how it . . . works in your . . . movies?"

"Yea, you got me there."

Evey turned to Alex. "And you—where's the brave cousin who . . . wanted to . . . to fight the East Siders?"

"Um . . ." Alex mumbled. "You're right. I'm in."

"Okay," Evey said, "then let's get . . . Howie."

Evey, Archer, and Alex walked over to their families to grab Howie and say goodbye. With Grandpa's help, they had convinced their parents to let them sail to Coyote Island to "watch the fireworks." Grandpa also loaned them some supplies.

"Remember, there's a storm coming later tonight, so be back at the house by eleven," Evey's mom said. "And make sure to check in with Grandpa on the walkie-talkies when you get there."

"They'll be fine," Grandpa said. "I added the sidelights to the boat, so no worries about the dark. And besides, Evey's a great sailor!" Grandpa winked at Evey.

Evey winked back. She looked at the end of the bridge where the *Sunrise* was docked. The small, red and green sidelights on the hulls gave the boat a dim glow.

185

"I'll be on channel eight," Grandpa said. "Give me a holler when you're there."

Evey nodded, then headed to the end of the bridge with Archer, Alex, and Howie.

"How long until the fireworks?" Archer asked.

"Twenty minutes," Evey said. She looked at Alex as he struggled to snap Howie's life vest on. "Need . . . help?"

Alex hugged Howie to stop him from running away. "He doesn't seem to like this," Alex grumbled.

Evey helped hold Howie down so Alex could secure the life vest. When they finished, Howie stood up, whimpered, and took several awkward steps toward the water.

Archer pet Howie. "I've never seen a dog life vest before. Is it supposed to fit like that?"

Alex laughed. "Don't let him fool you. He's worn it plenty of times. My grandma used to put doggles on him too."

"Doggles?" Archer asked as he watched Howie try to scratch his ear.

"Yes, as in dog goggles," Alex said.

"Why did you not bring those?" Archer asked. "Howie probably looks like an attack dog with them on!"

Alex shook his head while Howie rubbed his ear on the ground.

"On the boat," Evey said. "We need to . . . to go."

The four walked down the rocks between the water and the end of the bridge. Evey jumped on first and began prepping the sails. Archer and Alex helped Howie on before boarding themselves.

"Does everybody . . . have . . . their life vests?" Evey asked. Alex and Archer nodded. "Let's check our . . . supplies," she continued.

Archer sorted through the backpack. "Walkie-talkies, Alex's phone, flashlight, rope, compass, water-tight bags, water bottles, and a hammer—for some reason." He took the hammer out and held it up. "You planning on rebuilding the lighthouse once we find it?"

Evey laughed, then started untying the boat from the rocks.

"I still feel like we're forgetting something," Archer said. Evey and Alex both shrugged.

"Why are you bringing that?" Alex asked while pointing to the blue badminton racquet slung across Archer's back.

"You mean *Blue Steel*," Archer replied.

"It has a name?" Alex said.

"All of my racquets do. And the better question is why don't you have one. We're going to a jungle island controlled by a gang of angry kids. Oh, and let's not forget— a pirate and his army of dead coyotes probably haunt the place."

Alex rolled his eyes. "What are you going to do—hit a badminton birdie at them?"

"You'll see," Archer said as he tightened the strap attached to his racquet.

Evey ignored their banter and focused on the boat. She raised the sails and tied down the boom, then worked the rudder to steer the *Sunrise* away from the bridge. She headed south and stuck close to the shore to stay out of the East Siders' view. After a few minutes, she switched places with

Archer so he could control the rudder while she worked the sails.

"Turn us to port," Evey said. "Head . . . southeast."

Archer held out the compass and maneuvered the rudder so the boat turned toward Coyote Island. Evey adjusted the sails. They picked up speed and closed on the island quickly.

"Is that the cliff?" Alex asked once they could see the root-covered rock wall.

Evey nodded.

"I hate to question your plan, Evey, but how are we getting Howie up that thing? It must be almost ten feet tall."

Evey winked at Alex. As they approached the island, she dropped the sails while Archer steered the boat toward the rock wall. Alex tied a rope to one of the dangling tree trunks hanging over the water. Once Evey finished with the sails, she slung the backpack around her shoulders and grabbed a tree root.

"Alex, follow me," Evey said as she started climbing. Alex grabbed another root and began pulling himself up. Evey reached the top first and slung her feet over the edge. She rolled the rest of her body onto the ground, then turned to help Alex. "See, no problem," she said.

"For us," Alex said, "but what about Howie?"

Evey pointed to the boat, where Archer was securing a rope to Howie's life vest. "Ready for the rope?" Archer asked.

Evey nodded. Archer coiled the rope and threw it to her. She caught it and wrapped it around a large branch above her head to use as a pulley. "Time to pull," she said to Alex.

"You've got to be kidding me," he said. "Grandpa would not be happy with this."

"Why do—I mean . . . who do you . . . think gave me the idea?" Evey said as she pulled.

"Seriously?" Alex said as he tugged. "Speaking of Grandpa, what does he feed Howie? He weighs a ton!"

The two put all of their weight into pulling the rope. Still on the boat, Archer held Howie's belly to help lift him. After a few more pulls, Howie's confused face appeared over the edge of the cliff. Evey held the rope steady while Alex snatched Howie's vest and pulled him to the ground. Archer came up soon after. The three took off their life vests and hid them in the bushes. Alex removed Howie's, who then busied himself sniffing the trees. Evey, Archer, and Alex huddled together.

"Ouch!" Archer said as he slapped his arm.

"What?" Alex said.

"A mosquito bit me—I knew we forgot something!"

Evey rolled her eyes. She opened her mouth to speak, but a sudden blast of wind from the lake nearly knocked her over. She grabbed a tree trunk to steady herself.

"That's not a good sign," Archer said as he adjusted his Bears hat.

"Now what?" Alex asked.

"We're on a haunted island searching for the key to Evey's magical crystal's secret. That wind gust was definitely supernatural!"

"It's just the storm you illogical, paranoid—"

"Focus," Evey cut in. "Alex, you tay here with . . . Howie. Wait for my . . . signal."

"Sure," Alex said, "but what am I supposed to do if the East Siders find me?"

"Tell Howie to play . . . guard dog. He sounds . . . ferocious."

Archer looked at Howie, who was rubbing his back on a tree trunk. "Howie's ferocious?"

"He's got a decent bark," Alex said.

"We should be back toon—I mean . . . soon," Evey continued. "Hopefully, before the fire . . . works . . . stop."

"Speaking of those," Archer said. He looked at the dark sky. "Shouldn't they start right about—"

Boom! A bright green light lit the sky. Evey looked up through the trees and saw a massive firework to the east. For a few seconds, everything around them glowed green.

"We need to . . . hurry," Evey said. "Alex, let Grandpa know we—"

Bang! A second firework exploded, giving the trees a yellow glow. Alex took out his walkie-talkie and waved to Evey and Archer as they started walking through the thick woods to reach the clearing. Archer led the way, using his racquet to clear a path. Evey followed with the compass to make sure they stayed on an eastward heading. With the fireworks exploding overhead, the woods around them changed between shades of red, yellow, orange, green, blue, and purple.

"I feel like I'm at a dance party," Archer said.

Evey smiled, but kept her eyes down to avoid tripping. The fireworks provided just enough light to see the roots and branches covering the ground. After a few minutes of hiking, she noticed the dense woods thinning.

Boom! Boom! Boom! Evey looked up as a series of fireworks exploded overhead and sent purple sparks across the sky. She followed the light down until it covered the island, then saw the clearing ahead.

"We made it," Archer whispered.

Evey nodded while she studied the clearing. Waist-high grass covered it from one end to the other. She saw no sign of the East Siders.

Archer crouched next to Evey. "What's our next move?" he asked.

"Walk around the edge," Evey said. "See if . . . something ticks out."

"Let's stay low in case the East Siders are hiding. Hopefully, the fireworks are keeping them busy."

Evey and Archer scurried along the edge of the trees. They moved north toward the thin end of the clearing.

Bang! Bang! Another loud set of fireworks exploded overhead and rained down red and purple sparkles. The glow revealed a large tree at the end of the clearing. When Evey saw it, she stopped so suddenly Archer smacked into her, knocking them both to the ground.

"Ouch," Archer grumbled. He brushed the dirt off his shirt and stood up. "What's the deal?"

Evey clutched her crystal. "That . . . tree," she said. "It looks . . . familiar."

Boom! Boom! Boom! Three fireworks exploded, helping Evey see the tree clearly. It was short, but had a wide trunk. Only a few leaves clung to its branches, which stuck out to the left and right in a mangled fashion.

Archer turned to Evey. "That ugly thing," he said. "What about it?"

"I . . . climbed it . . . in . . . vision," Evey said.

"Huh—" Before Archer could say more, Evey jogged to the tree and pulled herself up the lowest branch. "I'm not even going to ask," Archer said as he followed.

Evey climbed over ten feet, then surveyed the clearing.

Archer followed her up. "Good thinking," he said. "We can see the whole clearing up here."

Evey felt a brush of cold air hit her back and neck. She turned to check the woods behind her. *Were those yellow eyes?* she thought as she tried to see through the tree branches. She leaned forward for a better look, but another gust of wind blew through the island. The tree shook violently back-and-forth. Evey and Archer wrapped themselves around the trunk until the shaking stopped. Once the tree steadied, Evey looked back at the woods, but saw nothing.

"Or maybe not such a good idea," Archer said. "You know, now that I think about it, I never liked climbing trees. When I was little, at a Labor Day party at a park, I saw this kid fall out of one. An ambulance had to take him away and—"

"Archer," Evey whispered, "I think you're . . . nervous."

"Sorry. It's just that we're searching an island in the dark based on visions from your haunted crystal. Sitting in a dead, monster-looking tree. Creepy gusts of wind. Just an average day, I guess."

Evey's focus broke. She blurted out a loud laugh, then immediately covered her mouth.

"Do you want to tell the East Siders we're here?" Archer said with a smirk.

Evey raised her eyebrow.

"We're adventurers, Evey. Put on your serious face," Archer said. "Anyway, what are we looking for? I don't see any touristy road signs saying 'lighthouse this way.'"

Evey smiled. "I think the . . . lighthouse was on a . . . small hill."

The two scanned the clearing for a minute. "Nothing looks hilly to me," Archer said. "The grass is too tall to tell."

"Keep trying," Evey said. She rubbed her crystal as she looked over the clearing. She took a deep breath and closed her eyes. She tried to remember the details of her visions. She saw the island's tall grass waving in the wind. She saw herself sitting in the tree. She felt the cold rain and wind. She saw the bright light from the lighthouse. She kept her eyes fixed on the light until it finally passed over her. She saw the small stone and wooden lighthouse sitting next to the boulders.

Pop! Pop! Pop! More fireworks flew across the sky, snapping Evey out of her daze. She looked back at the clearing, now covered in a red glow. She held out a finger and traced a path from the tree to the spot where she saw the lighthouse in her vision.

"Right there," Evey said as she pointed near the middle of the clearing.

"Where?" Archer asked. "I don't see anything."

"Trust me."

"Okay, vision master, lead the way."

Evey and Archer climbed down the tree. They dangled from the lowest branch and dropped to the ground.

Another gust of wind blew through the island. Cold air swept over Evey's back and up her neck, raising the hairs across her body. She shivered as she turned back to the woods to search for yellow eyes.

Nothing, Evey thought as she stared at the thick maze of trees. She watched them sway back-and-forth. The loud rustling of their leaves nearly blocked the noise from the fireworks. *I think Archer's rambling is rubbing off on me.*

Archer took a deep breath. "I'm not even going to say anything this time," he said.

Evey raised her eyebrow again.

"Hey," Archer said, "you won't be raising that eyebrow when the zombie Coyote Pirate shows up wanting his crystal back. Haven't you ever seen a scary movie? Random wind gusts are never a good sign!"

"I'd be more . . . worried about coyotes," Evey mumbled as she started walking into the clearing.

"Don't even start with the coyotes, Evey!"

"Shush!" Evey said.

"Oh, right. Quiet and sneaky. Not like the East Siders can hear us over the fireworks. Speaking of which . . ."

Evey and Archer both looked at the sky. The fireworks exploded three, four, sometimes five at a time. Sparks of all different colors streaked in every direction. The constant booms reminded Evey of a thunderstorm. *The finale*, she thought.

"We only have a few minutes—hurry!" Archer yelled.

The two ran through the tall grass. The constant barrage of fireworks gave Evey enough light to focus on the spot she saw in the tree. After a minute of running, she skidded to a stop. Archer plowed into her, but managed to stop from falling.

"Stop that!" Archer said.

Evey shrugged, then scanned their surroundings. "We're close," she said.

The two walked around the area. "Evey, over here," Archer said. "This little mound. It's not much, but you said the lighthouse was on a small hill."

Evey looked at the small mound. A thick pile of vines and weeds covered it, and several boulders laid next to it. *Those rocks—I saw those,* she thought.

Archer walked up the mound and started pulling the viny weeds. "Maybe there's something underneath this junk," he said.

"Careful," Evey said.

"What, it's just a bunch of—"

Thump! Archer fell through the weeds and disappeared.

CHAPTER 24

"**A**rcher!" Evey yelled. She heard nothing in response except the fireworks overhead. She crawled up the mound of weeds and peeked in the hole.

"Hey!" Archer said as he popped his head up, nearly hitting Evey.

"Ah!" she screamed.

"Oh, sorry," Archer said. "This hole is only a few feet deep. Hurt like heck, though. I don't have a concussion or anything, but I think I sprained my ankle. I hope I didn't tear anything. My friend's dad is a foot doctor and he says ankle tears are—"

"Archer!" Evey yelled.

"What are you yelling at me for? I'm the one with the mangled ankle!"

"Can you . . . walk?"

Archer took a few steps. "Yea, it's just sore."

"I'm just glad . . . you're alright. I don't know . . . what I'd—" Evey stopped talking when she noticed Archer looking at her. With her lying on the ground and Archer standing up in the hole, their faces were right next to each other. *Why is he staring at me?* she wondered.

"Hey, Evey," Archer said quietly. He leaned closer.

Oh no—what's he doing? Evey thought. Her jaw tightened. *Is he going to try to kiss me? Quick, say something about the lighthouse. Say anything!* "Yea?" she mumbled.

"I don't know why it took me so long to realize this, but you have three moles on your cheek that look like the Triforce."

Evey sighed and sat up. She looked at the barrage of fireworks still going off in the sky. *Should I be relieved or annoyed?* she thought.

"That's a compliment you know," Archer said. "The Triforce represents power, wisdom, and courage. I wish I had one on my face."

Evey rolled her eyes. *Does everybody play this game but me?* she thought.

Archer felt around for a strong weed to pull himself out of the hole. "Did any of your visions include random holes in the ground?" he asked.

"No, but . . ." Evey opened the backpack and took out the flashlight. She pointed it at the hole and turned it on. Behind the weeds and vines, she saw gray stones. She handed the flashlight to Archer and swung her feet into the hole. "Can you . . . help me down?" she asked.

"Down?" Archer said. "How about you help me up. Aren't we looking for a lighthouse?"

Evey dropped into the hole. "Archer, this is the . . . lighthouse."

Archer looked at the hole surrounding him. "I'm no expert, but I'm pretty sure lighthouses are above ground."

Evey ripped away a large section of the vines and weeds lining the hole, revealing a wall of stones. She shined the flashlight on it. "See it now?" she asked.

Archer felt the stones. "Is this some kind of cellar?"

Evey nodded.

"But if the actual lighthouse is gone, where's the secret?" Archer asked.

"Remember the last line in . . . the . . . letter to Evelyn?" Evey asked.

"No. Should I?"

"It didn't say to . . . look *in* the . . . lighthouse. It said to look . . . *beneath* it." Evey ripped more of the weeds and vines away. Archer helped her until they cleared most of the walls.

"It's definitely some type of tiny cellar," Archer said. He spread his arms across and almost touched both sides at the same time. "I guess we're beneath the lighthouse. Do you see any secrets lying around?"

Evey was busy feeling the stones.

"Now what are you doing?" Archer asked.

"Checking for loose tones . . . stones. I think . . . there's a . . . hidden room."

Archer pulled the hammer from the backpack. "Is that why you brought this?"

Evey nodded and grabbed the hammer.

"Do you feel anything?" Archer asked.

"Everything feels . . . solid," Evey said.

"What about airflow?"

Evey raised her eyebrow.

"You know, like in adventure movies. Sometimes, you can feel air going in or out of a secret room. Like through these gaps in the mortar." Archer pointed to the large cracks between some of the stones.

"That's a . . . thing?" Evey asked.

"It is in movies. Let's try it."

Starting on opposite sides of the cellar, the two felt for air flowing between the stones. Evey moved her hands up and down, then stopped when she felt a slight tickle. "Like this?" she asked.

Archer handed the flashlight to Evey and felt the area she pointed to. "Maybe," he said. "Let me see the hammer." Evey handed it to him. He used the claw end to break up the loose pieces of mortar. After wiping them away, he felt the stones again. "Whoa," he said, "there's definitely air coming through there."

"Let's ham . . . hammer before the . . . fireworks . . . stop," Evey said.

"Okay, watch out," Archer said.

Evey pulled herself out of the cellar. She sat on the edge and held the flashlight so Archer could see. He held the hammer in a downward position as if golfing one-handed. He brought it back, then swung it forward until it crashed into the stones. The constant fireworks blocked the noise. Archer took more swings, sending small pieces of stone and mortar flying in every direction. A large stone started to wobble. Archer nailed it a few more times until it fell backward, revealing a small, black hole in the side of the cellar wall. Tired and sweating, he dropped the hammer and fell to his knees to take a look.

"Can you . . . see anything?" Evey asked as she slid back into the cellar.

"No, it's all black. And it smells like my dad's gym bag."

Bang! Bang! Bang! Three fireworks exploded overhead, giving the island a yellow glow. After a few seconds, the light faded and the island turned dark.

199

"The fireworks are over," Archer whispered.

Evey nodded, then slowly stood up to check the clearing. Without the fireworks, the area looked nearly black. She could not see much through the tall grass, but a sound in the distance caught her attention. "Voices," she whispered.

"Help me," Archer said. He moved to a seated position and started kicking the stones around the hole.

Evey sat down and joined him. With each kick, the stones wobbled. Two, then three more fell behind the wall. Above the cellar, the voices grew louder. Evey recognized one as Finn's.

Hurry! Evey thought. She bent her legs, took a deep breath, and kicked as hard as she could. A pile of stones collapsed with a series of thuds, revealing a large hole in the cellar wall. Evey grabbed Archer by the shoulder and they dove through it.

Evey crashed onto a hard floor, scraping her hands. *Yuck, it does smell like a gym bag in here*, she thought as she pulled herself up to her knees. She and Archer sat still and listened to the voices outside. Evey touched the damp floor. It felt like a mixture of crushed stone and mud. Still crouching, she reached up and felt the ceiling right above her head.

"Jeez," Archer said once the voices trailed off, "that was close."

"Do you . . . have the . . . flash . . . light?" Evey asked.

"I thought you had it," Archer said. "Feel around. It has to be here somewhere."

The two searched for the flashlight on their hands and knees. "Ouch!" they muttered after bumping heads.

Archer rubbed above his eyes. "I wouldn't have signed up for this if I knew I would need to visit the hospital afterward."

Evey chuckled. "Keep looking," she said.

"Got it," Archer said after a minute. "Never mind. It's just a stick—a slimy one. Gross."

"Found it," Evey said. She lifted the flashlight off the ground and turned it on. "Ah!" she screamed as the light revealed a monstrous face on the wall. She dropped the flashlight and stumbled backward.

"Why did you shine that in my face?" Archer asked.

"Huh?" Evey said. She picked up the flashlight and pointed it toward Archer's voice. He was rubbing his eyes. Gray mud covered his arms, head, and Bears hat. Evey started laughing.

"What's so funny?" Archer asked. "You nearly blinded me."

"Look at . . . yourself," Evey said.

Archer looked at his mud-covered arms. "Yikes," he said.

"I thought you . . . were a . . . zombie!"

"What do you look like?" Archer took the flashlight and pointed it at Evey. The same gray mud covered her body, face, and red hair. She held her arms straight out and grimaced.

"I told you we'd run into zombies," Archer said as he wiped the mud off his face.

Evey laughed. "Let's see . . . what's in . . . here." She took the flashlight and moved it around. They were in a long tunnel. Evey guessed it was only about four feet high and five feet wide. The same stones from the cellar lined the walls. Large, wooden beams framed the ceiling. Grass roots stuck through the mortar.

"Wow," Archer said. "How far does this thing go?"

"Let's . . . find out," Evey said as she started crawling.

Archer followed. "Do you think this thing is stable? These wood beams don't exactly look to be in the best shape. I think they're rotted. I hope this place doesn't collapse. I knew a kid whose grandpa worked in a mine when it collapsed. He said—"

"Archer," Evey cut in.

"Sorry. I know, it's just nerves. I'm sure it's safe in here. But I've seen some home renovation shows. You're supposed to have an engineer make sure walls are not load bearing before you knock them—"

"Archer!"

"I'm just kidding—I hope."

Evey turned back to the far side of the tunnel. "Keep moving. I see . . . something."

"I feel like we've crawled a mile down here," Archer said.

Evey pointed the flashlight at the hole leading outside. "I think . . . we've gone maybe . . . fifteen feet," she said.

Archer looked back. "Oh, that actually makes me feel better." Evey turned to continue crawling, but Archer grabbed her shoulder. "Hang on a second," he said. "Can you point the flashlight by me?"

Evey shined the light at Archer while he looked through the backpack and grabbed the walkie-talkie.

"Better be safe than sorry," Archer said. He hit the speak button and the walkie-talkie's green light turned on. "Alex, this is Archer. Can you hear me?" Archer let go of the button. He turned up the volume, but only heard static. "Alex, are you there?"

"What did you say?" said a groggy-sounding Alex.

Evey and Archer looked at each other. "Was he sleeping?" Archer said. He hit the talk button. "Were you sleeping, Alex?"

"Um, no," Alex said.

Evey and Archer shook their heads. "Whatever," Archer said. "I just wanted to check in to make sure everything is okay out there."

"Yea, me and Howie are fine. He's asleep—I mean, guarding things."

"Sounds like you're really on top of things, Alex. Me and Evey are crawling through a really old, secret tunnel in the center of the island. If you don't hear from us in about twenty minutes, call for help."

"Um, okay," Alex said. "You know, we could've just played a board game tonight."

Archer shook his head again as he put the walkie-talkie back in the backpack. "At least Howie can try to find us if we get stuck down here," he said.

Evey turned the light back toward the end of the tunnel and continued crawling. "There's . . . something," she said.

They crawled a few more feet until they reached the end. Evey pointed the flashlight at a small, wooden chest. She guessed it measured eighteen inches across. Rusted metal hinges covered the corners. Two latches sealed it shut.

"Whoa," Archer said as he crouched next to Evey. "It literally looks like a tiny treasure chest."

"What . . . were you . . . expecting?" Evey asked.

"Honestly, the Coyote Pirate's skeleton," Archer said. "This looks way better, thankfully. But do you actually think—it couldn't really be, could it? I guess I just assumed that we wouldn't really find . . ."

Archer's words faded away as Evey stared at the chest. Her head felt heavy. Her field of vision narrowed. She slowly extended her hand and touched the chest. A series of images flashed through her mind. She saw herself holding a lantern. She placed something in the chest. The sound of howling filled the air. She slammed the chest shut and raced out of the tunnel and into the lighthouse.

"Evey, you okay?" Archer asked.

"What?" she said as she shook her head.

"You zoned out again. Do you know you do that a lot?"

Evey shrugged.

"So, do you think this could be it?" Archer asked. "The key to finding the secret? It has to be, right?"

Evey rubbed her eyes as she tried to process what she just saw. "I think . . . we're on the . . . right track," she said. She reached for the latches.

"Wait!" Archer said as he grabbed Evey's hand. "I just want to say that if we unleash a curse by opening this, I'm blaming you."

Evey laughed. *It'll be fine—probably*, she thought. She tried to open the latches, but they did not budge. "Ugh," she said as she leaned back from the chest.

"Is it locked?" Archer asked.

"I don't . . . think so. Maybe the latches are . . . stuck . . . from the rust."

Archer dug through the backpack. "Watch out," he said as he pulled the hammer out. Evey moved aside. Archer held the chest down and hit each latch a few times. "Try now."

Evey grabbed the latches again. Both flipped up, unsealing the chest.

"Are you ready?" Archer asked.

Evey nodded. She and Archer each held a side of the chest and counted together, "One . . . two . . . three!"

Evey and Archer opened the lid. A rush of dusty air blew in their faces. They both turned away and coughed. After wiping her eyes, Evey looked into the chest. She could barely see, so she reached in and pulled out the first thing she felt.

CHAPTER 25

Archer rubbed his eyes. "What is it?" he asked.

Evey brought the item close to her face. "It's a . . . a book. Like a . . . journal."

"A journal?" Archer said. "Is the cover made of valuable crystals?"

Evey put the journal in her lap and shined the flashlight on it. She brushed off a layer of dust to reveal a worn, brown leather cover. A string held it closed. "Remember, Archer," she said, "this is . . . supposed to *lead* us to . . . the secret."

"Doesn't that seem unnecessarily complicated to you?" Archer said. "Why not just hide everything in the same place? It's like when shows drag things out so they can keep making new seasons. If you ask me, the Coyote Pirate is starting to sound like a writer making a pitch to some . . ."

Evey zoned out as she felt the journal's cover. *I feel like I've held this before*, she thought.

"Evey, you okay?" Archer asked.

"Uh . . . yea," she said. "Just . . . trying to open it."

"It looks pretty simple. Unless there's a spell we need to recite to prevent it from waking the army of dead pirates."

Evey laughed. *Curses or not, here we go*, she thought. She carefully untied the string and opened the cover. The stiff, yellowed first page had only a few words written on it. It crinkled as Evey pressed her fingers on it.

Archer squinted and leaned forward. "I can't believe people always wrote in this fancy cursive. It's like the Christmas cards I get from my aunt. I can barely read them. Honestly, I think she just does it to show off her—sorry, I'm rambling again."

Evey rubbed her eyes. "I think it says, 'A record by Oliver . . . Solborg—Keeper of the Coyote Bay . . . Lighthouse.'"

"Oliver Solborg," Archer repeated. "Sounds Norwegian to me."

"It makes . . . sense," Evey said.

"That the Coyote Pirate was Norwegian?"

"No," Evey said a she shook her head. "The letter to Evelyn was . . . signed 'O~G.' He was using . . . his initial."

"Wouldn't his initials be O.S.?"

"Oh, you're right," Evey said. She looked at the journal. "G is the last letter in . . . Solborg. And . . . remember how he wrote . . . that curvy line between . . . the letters."

"Oh, yea," Archer said. "I guess you usually write your initials right next to each other. Maybe it was supposed to be like a blank line so that Evelyn could fill in the rest. Kind of clever actually, but it still seems like a boring name for the Coyote Pirate."

"It's no . . . Cheesebeard," Evey said with a smirk.

Archer laughed. "Exactly."

Evey turned the page, revealing a journal entry with small writing. "I can barely . . . hard to read in the . . . dark." She flipped through the journal's hundreds of pages. "This is going to take . . . forever," she said.

"Let's just read the beginning and the end," Archer said. "Like I do for my book reports."

Evey raised her eyebrow.

"What?" Archer said. "The middle is usually just fluff. Take this whole adventure—wouldn't it have been better if your first vision just told you to come here? Instead, we had to go through a book's worth of stuff in the middle."

Evey rolled her eyes and turned back to the journal. She found the first entry and read it aloud with Archer:

> February 23rd, 1845
>
> I have reached nearly two years in my position as keeper of the Coyote Bay lighthouse. My work until now has proven pleasant, but uneventful. However, recent events of great importance have encouraged me to begin journaling my experiences for the sake of maintaining a proper record.
>
> Last year, I began communicating with natives of the local Potawatomi tribe, whose village lies just north of Coyote Bay. After some initial awkwardness on both sides, I have been able to develop an excellent relationship with them. They find my work very interesting. They refer to the lighthouse with a word I believe best translates to "sunrise."

"Sunrise—there it is!" Archer said. "Your vision was right!"

Evey nodded. *I guess I'm not losing my mind,* she thought. *Although, I don't know if seeing a dead pirate's memories is any better.*

"Although," Archer continued, "it's kind of scary that you really are having visions of a dead pirate's memories. I haven't actually stopped to think about that until now."

Evey glared at Archer. *Not helping!* she thought.

"Sorry, I shouldn't have said that out loud," Archer said. "It's probably fine. If you need to, you can always toss the crystal back in the lake."

Evey rubbed her temples. *Maybe I should've brought Alex down here instead so he could tell me this is all a coincidence,* she thought.

"So, anyway—let's keep reading." Archer turned back to the journal:

> I have been fortunate to join the Potawatomi on several excursions across the peninsula, giving me an opportunity to view much of this land's inspiring scenery. The natural beauty here reminds me of Norway's great fjords.

"Ha! I told you he was Norwegian," Archer said.

Evey smiled. *That actually is really impressive,* she thought. She continued reading:

> Most stunning among them, I encountered a great bluff at the top of a waterfall. A strange but comforting feeling overtook me when in its presence, as if I was a lost child finding his mother. In the sunlight, the waterfall looks golden. In the moonlight, it looks as if it glows. This Moonlight Bluff lies at the end of the creek that feeds into the north end of Coyote Bay.

"Wait," Archer said, "did we just find the secret on the first page—Moonlight Bluff?"

"I tink so," Evey mumbled.

"And it even gave us the directions! I told you we could just skim this thing. Mystery solved!" Archer raised his hand for a high-five, but saw a few tears trickling down Evey's cheeks. "You okay?" he asked.

Evey nodded. "I just . . . I can't believe we bound . . . found it." She wiped her eyes. "I teal appy—I mean . . . happy. Good to know . . . this is . . . it's . . ."

"Real?" Archer asked.

Evey shook her head yes.

"I for one always believed in you," Archer said. "I don't know about Alex, though. I still think he only came along because he's bored without his Legos."

Evey laughed and smiled at Archer. He smiled back, and the two suddenly leaned forward and hugged. After a few seconds, they pulled apart. "Tarry," Evey said. She bit her lip.

Archer's face turned red enough to show through the mud. "Um . . ." he mumbled while squirming. "That was awkward. Not because of you—it's just—sorry."

"That did feel weird," Evey said. *Oh no, I said that out loud! Say something else!* "I mean, not . . . weird-weird, just—uh . . . read more."

The two turned back to the journal:

> Unfortunately, the loggers and their ships that use this lighthouse as a guide seem to care little for this natural beauty, or for the welfare of the Potawatomi and other settlers who rely on these lands. To the contrary, they

wish to log the lands north of the lake. This will destroy an important ecosystem, and threaten Moonlight Bluff.

I have heard discussions among the loggers about these lands for some time. However, only recently have they begun citing the Indian Removal Act, the cruel law that has forced countless natives from their homes.

Consequently, I decided I will seek to negotiate a truce with the loggers. Such an agreement will ideally prevent any violence. I hope we can find a way to share this wonderful land.

Archer leaned back. "That's one heck of a first journal entry. And I guess it proves our theory. The Coyote Pirate wasn't trying to escape with treasure. He—Oliver—really was protecting this Moonlight Bluff. But I wonder where your crystal fits in."

"I'm guessing we need to . . . keep reading," Evey replied.

"Right, let's go to the end."

Evey flipped through the journal until she came across the last entry. The two read it together:

September 2nd, 1851

I fear my efforts to protect this peninsula have failed. Most of the Potawatomi have been forced to leave, and I just received word that a group of loggers intend to march through the forest around Moonlight Bluff to evict the remaining settlers who live there. Ever since Door County was formally organized earlier this year, I feared such an action.

I must do something to protect Moonlight Bluff. If the loggers clear these woods, they will destroy a magical ecosystem. Let there be no mistake that Moonlight Bluff is special. Magical, spiritual, mystical, whatever it may be, there is some power there. One only need to visit it to know. Watch the crystals glow in the moonlight.

Evey grabbed her crystal. *Watch the crystals glow in the moonlight,* she repeated to herself. She squeezed her fingers as she continued reading:

> I do not pretend to fully understand this power. But I do know that such things should be respected. Moonlight Bluff seems to forge a connection with the supernatural world. I feel this connection when I hold a crystal. I see it in the dreams and visions that trouble my sleep.
>
> Destroying this place would be a tragedy. More distressing, I fear a danger exists if someone learns to harness this power. I am not sure how, but I fear it could be used for something evil. I cannot allow this to happen. I must try to stop them.

Archer turned to Evey. "That can't be the end," he said. "What happened next?" Archer flipped through the journal, but the remaining pages were all blank. "There's got to be more!"

"Strange," Evey mumbled.

"I know. I mean, how does it end on a cliffhanger like that? Did the Coyote Pirate lose his hand and get a hook that he couldn't write with?"

"No," Evey said through a laugh. "The last line—'I must try to . . . stop them.' That's . . . familiar."

"Well, I'm officially confused," Archer said. "Maybe this would make sense if you were the Evelyn from the museum's letter."

Evey nodded. "I think we need to read more . . . than the beginning and end."

"I'll let you handle that," Archer said as he set the journal down and closed it. "Like I said—"

A cold gust of wind whipped through the cellar and into the tunnel. Evey shivered as the chilly air ran up her back. She watched the journal's pages flip in the wind until it settled on an entry with a drawing. Evey pushed her tangled, muddy hair away from her eyes to take a look, but Archer gasped and grabbed her arm.

"What!" Evey yelled.

Archer took a deep breath. "I think that creepy gust of wind just turned the journal to a very important page," he said.

Evey raised her eyebrow.

"Just look," Archer said.

Evey rolled her eyes and picked up the journal. A rough sketch of a person filled the top of the page. It was a young girl with short, red hair.

"Did you see the picture?" Archer asked. Evey, her eyes fixed on the page, slowly nodded. "Am I crazy, or does it look like you?" Archer continued. "It could be a coincidence, right—where's Alex when you need him—because if it's not a coincidence, then I think you somehow . . ."

Evey did not hear Archer as her eyes drifted to the bottom of the page to read the journal entry:

August 16th, 1850

I had another strange dream last night. If it even was a dream. Whereas previously I always saw my sister or the kindly, red-haired woman on the island, this time it was a peculiar young lady. I tried to speak with her, but it seems everything I said just made her raise an eyebrow.

Evey froze. The journal fell from her hands and smacked the ground with a thud.

"So, not a coincidence," Archer said. "That's kind of what I figured."

Evey turned to Archer. "He . . . he . . ." She rubbed her jaw.

"What is it!"

"How . . . me . . ." Evey stopped trying to talk and picked up the journal. She shoved it in Archer's face.

Archer read the entry. "He had a dream about you—one hundred and seventy years ago. So, you are officially *that* Evelyn. And I am officially scared."

Evey looked at her crystal. "I don't tink . . . not dreams. It's like . . . we're—"

Screech! Archer dug the walkie-talkie out of the backpack and turned down the volume to quiet the static. He hit the talk button.

"Alex, was that you?" Archer said. He moved the walkie-talkie close to his ear to listen, but only heard static. "Alex, are you there?" The walkie-talkie returned static again. Archer turned to Evey. "I guess we better go before he calls the fire department to come save us. And I think it's gotten scary enough down here, anyway."

Evey nodded. She sealed the journal in a water-tight bag and put it in her backpack. She closed the chest, then followed Archer back to the tunnel entrance and into the lighthouse cellar.

The dim light from outside seemed unbearably bright compared to the dark tunnel. Evey squinted as she slowly stood up. The air felt much cooler, and the wind had picked up.

The storm's coming, Evey thought.

Splat! A paintball zipped by Evey's head and hit the back of the cellar. The paint splattered across her hair. She lost her balance and fell backward.

"I've had it with the paintballs!" Archer said as he tried to climb out of the cellar.

Splat! Another paintball hit his chest, knocking him down.

As Evey and Archer wiped the paint off themselves, Finn peered into the cellar with a large grin. "Did you say something?" he said.

CHAPTER 26

"Come on up," Finn said. "Show us what you found down there."

Evey ground her teeth as she glared at him. *You are not getting away this time*, she thought. She grabbed a handful of vines and pulled herself out of the cellar. Archer followed. Evey took a few deep breaths, then stood up.

"What's in your backpack?" Finn asked. Five other East Siders stood behind him.

"None of your business!" Archer yelled.

"I wasn't talking to you!" Finn shouted. He held up Evey's notebook. "I read your notes about the pirate guy you're obsessed with. I know you're looking for his secret treasure."

Finn threw the notebook to one of the East Siders guarding Archer. "You made it too easy for us," Finn continued. "A lighthouse on the island—we knew this had to be the place." Finn motioned to the cellar. "We thought about searching down there, but then we figured we could just wait for you two to do the work for us. And based on how you look, I think we made the right choice!" Finn high-fived one of the other East Siders. "Time to give it up," he said. "Hand over the backpack."

Evey shook her head no.

"Okay, we'll do it the hard way," Finn said. He reached for the backpack. Evey and Archer grabbed his hands and wrestled him to the ground. The other East Siders quickly pounced on them. Three of them dragged Archer away. The others helped Finn take the backpack from Evey.

"Knock it off, Finn!" Archer yelled.

"Shut up kid!" one of the East Siders said to Archer. They let him go, but one aimed the paintball gun at him.

Evey looked at Archer. He used his eyes to motion toward his pants pocket. Evey noticed the green light from the walkie-talkie barely sticking out of it. *I hope you're listening, Alex*, she thought.

"I'll give you this," Finn said as he inspected Evey's backpack, "you've got guts coming back here. But remember, this is our island. That makes this ours too."

Evey forced herself to stop grinding her teeth. *Start talking,* she thought. *Who cares what I sound like or if they make fun of me—they'll understand me.*

"You know, Finn," Archer said, "for somebody who's so strict about people not going near your island, you sure don't have a problem taking other people's stuff."

Finn nodded at the boy with the paintball gun. He shot at Archer's legs, splattering paint on his pants.

"I'll ask again," Finn said to Evey. "What did you find?"

Come on, Evey thought. *Remember what Grandpa said— everybody feels insecure, including Finn. That's why he acted weird at Chester's—why he ran away at the library.*

"Oh, I forgot—you don't talk," Finn said. "That's fine." He started opening the backpack.

"Hey, coward!" Archer yelled. Finn turned toward him. "Do you feel good picking on a girl? Do you think that makes you tough?"

Finn walked toward Archer. "What are you going to do," he said, "hit me with your racquet?"

"I don't need the racquet!" Archer yelled. "Not that it matters. I'm sure you wouldn't dare fight me by yourself. You need all your buddies here to help. I know about people like you. You act all tough to make yourself feel better because deep down inside, you're just scared!"

"Shut up!" Finn yelled as he shoved Archer to the ground. Archer stood back up and raised a fist.

"Stop!" Evey yelled. *Archer's right,* she thought. *Finn is scared. Time to give him something to be truly scared about.*

Everybody turned toward Evey. "You have something to say?" Finn asked.

You can do this, Evey thought. "We . . . we can't tay here," she said.

Finn smirked. "You don't have to *tay,*" he said. "We'll show you to the cliff and you can go *wimming* all the way home." The rest of the group laughed.

"I mean it!" Evey shouted. "We need to . . . leave."

Finn sighed. "Why?"

Evey took a deep breath. "The coyotes," she said.

The East Siders all laughed.

"I'm serious!" Evey shouted.

Finn walked over to Evey. "Coyotes—that's the best you can come up with?"

"Don't you ever ear—no . . . hear . . . them?" Evey asked.

The East Siders stopped laughing and turned to Evey.

"I do," she said. "I hear . . . howling late at night. I used to tink they . . . were coming from up . . . north. But now I know it's . . . here . . . on . . . this island." Evey noticed the East Siders were paying closer attention. She spoke louder. "Finn, don't you know . . . this island's name?"

Finn looked puzzled.

"Coyote Island," Evey said.

"What? I've never heard that," Finn said.

"I think that's true," said another East Sider. "It's some old legend, but I've heard it before."

Evey took a few steps toward Finn. "You've never . . . heard the tory?" she said.

Finn shook his head no. His eyes darted from left to right.

"Years ago," Evey continued, "during a bad . . . winter, a pack of . . . starving coyotes crossed the . . . frozen lake to come . . . here. They found plenty to eat, but they . . . stayed too long. A quick ring . . . spring . . . thawed the ice, and they were . . . trapped. Their food ran out, so the pack leader . . . tried to wim to shore, but . . . he drowned. The rest of the coyotes . . . howled for weeks until . . . they tarved. The island was quiet for a . . . while. But the . . . howling . . . started again years later. People . . . say it's from here. Say it's the . . . same coyotes."

Evey paused. She could see beads of sweat on Finn's forehead.

"That's garbage," Finn said. "We've been here dozens of nights. There are no coyotes—real or ghost."

"But you didn't . . . steal the Coyote Pirate's treasure," Evey said, pointing to the backpack.

A loud howl screamed through the air. Finn fell to the ground. The other East Siders jumped. The noise echoed through the trees around the clearing. The howl quieted, but started again, louder than the first time.

Evey stared at Finn's eyes. "Nobody's sure," she said. "They've . . . heard the howling, but is it . . . real? Some believe the Coyote Pirate trolled . . . controlled them. They say he used . . . them to protect his treasure. So, ask yourself—do you . . . think they're real?"

Another howl, louder and closer, echoed through the air. Finn's eyes darted all around. "Um . . ." he mumbled.

"One thing's for sure," Evey said. "They're . . . still . . . hungry!"

Something barked and growled at the edge of the clearing. One of the East Siders screamed. Another fell down.

"Archer, my notebook!" Evey yelled.

Archer took his racquet off his back and swung it at the East Sider holding Evey's notebook. It smashed his hand, knocking the notebook to the ground. The stunned East Sider ran across the clearing with the rest of his friends.

Evey and Finn both dove on the backpack. They wrestled back-and-forth as the barking grew louder. Evey clenched the backpack as hard as she could. "You're running out of time!" she yelled.

"Ah!" Finn screamed. He let go of the backpack, jumped to his feet, and ran away.

Evey fell backward with the backpack in her hands. *I can't believe that worked!* she thought. A few moments later, Howie ran up to her. "There's my good guard dog!" she said as she pet him. Howie licked her face, but quickly recoiled at the mud.

Alex jogged up behind Howie. "Did it work?" he asked.

"Yea," Archer said. "You weren't kidding. He does sound ferocious. And how did you get him to howl like that?"

Alex held up his phone. "Classical piano makes him howl, so I played a song for him. It's funny, but kind of creepy too."

"We're not out of diss yet," Evey said as she threw the backpack around her shoulders.

"Huh?" Alex said. "Didn't I just save the day? You two look terrible by the way. Did you take a mud bath?"

Evey pointed to the north edge of the clearing. Finn had stopped there and was staring at them.

"They know . . . we tricked them," Evey said. She started running toward the cliff. Archer and Alex followed with Howie.

"Did you even find the secret?" Alex yelled.

"Yes!" Evey said.

"What is it?"

"Too much to . . . explain! Just . . . run!"

Without the light from the fireworks, Evey could not see the ground. She tripped several times before she reached the path next to the cliff.

That's not good, Evey thought when she saw the water. With the storm approaching, the wind and waves had grown. The *Sunrise*, still tied to a tree, had drifted about fifteen feet from the cliff and bounced around in the choppy water.

Archer, Alex, and Howie slid to a stop behind Evey. Archer put his hands on his knees. "Badminton practice does not include enough cardio for this," he said between deep breaths.

Alex took a knee and pointed at the lake. "Can we sail in this?" he asked.

Evey smiled. The large waves reminded her of her last sailing lesson. *My parents did say this should be fun*, she thought.

"What do you think, Evey?" Archer asked.

"It's no worse tan my lessons," she said.

Archer shrugged. "I guess, but it looks scarier at night."

Evey pointed to the walkie-talkie in Archer's pocket. "If we need . . . help, we can call."

"You're right," Archer said. "Besides, we need to get that journal to safety."

"I believe in you, Evey," Alex said. He turned to Howie. "How about you, Howie?"

Howie slowly walked backward with a whimper.

"Oh, come on, big guy!" Alex said. "Our odds of dying aren't that high."

Archer laughed, then pointed to the *Sunrise*. "Now we just need to get the boat. Maybe I can climb down and work my way over to the rope."

Evey looked to the north. "We don't . . . have time."

"What?" Archer said as he tried to find a tree root to climb down. He and Alex looked in the same direction as Evey. In the distance, Finn's boat rounded the northwest corner of the island.

Evey turned back to the water. "We have to . . . jump."

CHAPTER 27

Archer and Alex both looked at the dark, choppy water and shook their heads no.

"We . . . have to," Evey said. She dug the life vests out of the bushes. "It's only a little . . . higher than the pier," she said as she put her vest on.

Alex snapped the clips on his life vest together. "Sure," he said, "like the pier at the beach. Except, at the pier we jumped into calm water in the daylight. That's exactly the same as this."

Evey ignored him as she secured Howie's life vest.

"Anybody want to go first?" Archer asked as he stared at the waves.

"Watch out!" Evey said. Archer and Alex turned to see her holding Howie like a giant baby.

"What are you—"

Evey rushed by with Howie huddled to her chest and leapt off the cliff. They hit the water with a giant splash. After a brief moment, both of them surfaced.

Why is this lake always freezing! Evey thought. She grabbed Howie's life vest and pulled him to the *Sunrise*.

Alex looked at Archer. "She'll never let us forget this if we don't do it," he said.

Archer nodded. "Okay, on three. One—"

"Now!" Alex yelled as he jumped. He tucked his legs into a cannonball as he fell to the water.

"Whatever," Archer mumbled. He followed with his own cannonball.

The two surfaced after a few seconds and swam to the *Sunrise*. Evey had already pulled herself and Howie onboard. She turned around and helped Alex and Archer.

"See, not too . . . bad," Evey said as she started untying the rope holding the boat to the tree.

"Just a fun dip in the lake," Archer said through chattering teeth.

"For the record," Alex said, "that's at least twice as high as the pier!"

Evey smiled as she finished untying the rope. "Archer, I'll . . . handle the . . . sails," she said. "You take the . . . the rudder. Alex, keep . . . Howie safe. It may get dumpy . . . bumpy."

"Hang on, big guy," Alex said as he huddled over Howie.

Archer turned to find Finn's boat. "Here they come," he said with a worried look. "Evey, are you sure about this?"

Evey nodded as she stared at Finn's boat. She raised the sails and set the boom. "Go southwest! Straight for . . . Grandpa's dock!"

Archer turned the rudder to steer them away from the cliff. The *Sunrise* took off in the strong wind. They cleared the southern tip of the island and lost the protection of its trees. The full force of the southeast wind hit the sails. The sudden gust pushed the port hull out of the water. Evey and Archer jumped to the left side of the boat to stop them from tipping over.

"Turn to board . . . starboard," Evey yelled once the boat stabilized. "Go west!"

Evey moved the boom to match Archer's steering, then looked behind her. Finn adjusted for the wind before she did, cutting the gap between them.

"They're gaining!" Archer shouted.

"I know!" Evey said. She kept the boat moving west as fast as possible, but Finn continued to close the distance. After a few minutes, the waves grew calmer as they neared the shoreline. Evey looked back at Finn's boat. She judged her lead was less than fifty feet.

"They're going to catch us!" Archer yelled.

Evey looked at Grandpa's dock. *Archer's right!* she thought. *We don't have enough time to dock.* She bit her lip as she tried to think of a plan. She closed her eyes and focused on the sound of her breathing to block out the noise from the wind and waves. Her mind flashed back to her vision of sailing the Coyote Pirate's boat in the storm. She saw the large ship chasing her. She heard the canon shots fly by. She felt the spray of the water across her face.

"Evey!" Alex yelled, snapping her out of her daze. "We can't fight them all off if they catch us. Any ideas?"

"Uh . . . yea," Evey said. "Alex, you know I . . . love you?"

"Huh?"

Evey turned to Archer. "Turn to port. Go south and . . . follow the . . . shore."

"Why aren't we heading for the dock?" Archer asked.

"Trust me."

Archer nodded and turned the boat. The dock now sat ahead of them, but off the starboard side.

"Alex," Evey said, "I need you and . . . Howie to . . . jump off."

"What!" Alex yelled. "Are you crazy?"

"I need to be . . . faster. We're too . . . heavy."

Alex glared at Evey.

"It's shallow," she said. "You can . . . walk in."

Alex continued glaring. "You better pack my suitcase for the rest of our lives!"

"Deal, but go now!" Grandpa's dock sat directly to the right of the boat.

Alex wrapped his arms around Howie. "Looks like we're swimming again," he said. Alex gave Evey one more glare, then rolled off the boat with Howie in his arms and splashed into the water.

"Wow, he really hates packing," Archer said.

Evey looked back to make sure Alex and Howie were safe. She saw them walking to shore. Further back, the East Siders slowed to a stop. Evey dropped her sails and lifted the backpack in the air.

"Finn, looking for diss!" Evey shouted across the water.

"That belongs to us!" Finn shouted back.

Evey threw the backpack on and tightened the straps. She pointed to the choppy water in the middle of the lake. "Come and get it!" She raised the sails and the boat jumped forward.

"We're going back out there?" Archer said.

Evey nodded.

"We can't outrun them forever," Archer said.

"We're through running from these punks," Evey said. She kneeled next to Archer. "Remember how the Coyote Pirate . . . dealt with people . . . chasing him."

Archer smiled. "I think I know what you have in mind, and I like it! Give me an order, Captain!"

"Head east, past Coyote Island to the . . . far shoreline."

"You got it!"

Evey looked back for Finn's boat. The confusion bought her some time. The East Siders were on the move again, but her lead had increased. As the *Sunrise* sailed into deeper water, the wind and waves grew. Cold water splashed into the boat, soaking Evey and Archer. She kept her focus on their surroundings as she maneuvered the sails to keep the boat stable. They reached the middle of the lake in a few minutes.

Evey turned back to see Finn's boat. He was closing the gap again. She wanted to beat him to the eastern shore before turning toward her target destination. However, she figured Finn would catch them before they made it.

"They're gaining!" Archer said.

"I know," Evey said. She looked at the flag on top of her mast. It still showed the strong wind coming from the southeast. *Fine—if I can't outrun Finn, I'll outmaneuver him!* she thought.

Evey turned back to Archer. "We need to go . . . southeast, into the . . . wind." She pointed to her destination on the far shore. "That bark . . . dark spot."

"This wind is brutal," Archer said. "How can we sail into it?"

"We tack," Evey replied. "Switch from . . . south to east. Go south . . . first." Archer and Evey worked together to turn the boat. They made the change smoothly and quickly. Evey looked back and saw that her plan worked. By the time Finn corrected his course to follow, her lead grew.

Evey maintained the south course for a couple of minutes. "Hard to port! Go . . . east!" she shouted to Archer.

The two worked in unison to navigate the turn. The *Sunrise* handled the wind and waves with ease, and cut through the water with increasing speed. They found a good rhythm tacking across the choppy lake and made several more turns. Evey smiled as Finn struggled to match her.

"Another turn, go east!" Evey shouted to Archer.

They turned the boat to port, but this time Finn predicted their move and matched it. His quick turn cut the distance between them.

Archer looked at the narrowing gap. "We have to speed up!" he yelled.

"The ails can't take it!" Evey shouted as she checked her stretched mainsail and jib. She wiped the water from her face and moved to the front of the boat. "One more . . . turn . . . now!"

The two turned the *Sunrise* one last time. Evey looked at Finn's boat. He again predicted her course and cut the distance between them. Evey judged his boat was only thirty feet behind.

Splat! Splat! Neon paint sprayed Archer and Evey. Archer wiped the paint from his legs. "Seriously, who even paintballs anymore!" he yelled.

Evey looked at Finn's boat. One of the East Siders was laying across the front with the paintball gun in hand. He struggled to fire shots in the choppy water, but managed to land a few on her sail. She turned back to the front of her boat.

"They're right on top of us!" Archer shouted.

Splat! Another paintball hit the sail.

Evey looked back. Finn's boat was so close she could see the grin on his face as he held the rudder. She turned forward again and finally spotted her destination—the large yard of Blacksmith Mansion.

"Over there!" Evey shouted to Archer as she pointed to a spot ahead of them. "Turn a little to . . . to port."

Archer turned the boat in the direction of Evey's arm.

"Get ready to . . . pull the rudder!" she said.

"Ready!" Archer said as he grabbed the rudder handle.

Evey looked over the side of the boat. She saw the sandy bottom through the shallow water. *Let's see if Finn knows this lake as well as I do*, she thought. "Now!" she yelled.

Archer lifted the two rudder blades out of the water. Evey felt a slight bump on the bottom of the *Sunrise* as they skimmed the sandbar. She turned to the East Siders and smiled at Finn just in time to see his grin change to a grimace. He jerked the rudder to turn his boat, but he was too late.

Finn's daggerboard smashed into the sandbar with a deep booming sound. The front of his boat lifted out of the water. It turned on its side and crashed against the sand with a loud thud, sending all six East Siders tumbling into the shallow water.

Once clear of the sandbar, Evey dropped the sails to slow down the *Sunrise*. Archer put the rudder blades down and turned them around to face the East Siders.

Finn smashed his hand in the water and glared at Evey and Archer. He opened his mouth to speak, but nothing came out.

Now he knows how I feel, Evey thought. She waved, raised the sails, and yelled "You can . . . follow the sandbar to . . . shore!"

"We did it!" Archer said as they left the East Siders behind. He and Evey hugged. After a few seconds, they pulled apart. Archer made a squeamish face. "That felt weird again," he said. "But not—"

Evey cut in. "Not beard-weird—I mean . . ." She put her face in her hands.

"Beard-weird?" Archer said with a smile. After a pause, he and Evey burst into laughter.

Yea Grandpa, Evey thought, *sometimes, those things are just funny.*

After Evey and Archer settled down, they stretched out across from each other on the trampoline. Still near the shore, the boat rocked gently in the smaller waves. Evey stared at the sky. The moon had risen, but was covered by the clouds. She pulled her crystal out from under her shirt.

"And to think," Archer said, "all I wanted to do this summer was practice badminton."

Evey shook her head. "What is with . . . this bad . . . badminton . . . tournament you keep talking about?"

"You mean *the* badminton tournament. It's the most important event of the year at my school. The winners are basically royalty."

"I thought my family's . . . Championship was . . . weird."

"I have to win this year," Archer said. "My sisters won when they were younger, so there's a lot of family pressure. They're twins, though, so it's not fair. Twins are impossible to beat in badminton. It's like they're one brain with two bodies. I don't think my partner and I will ever—"

A break in the clouds revealed the moon. Evey watched her crystal's red glow cover the *Sunrise*.

"Evey, your crystal!" Archer said.

She looked at the bright red light, then turned to Archer. "I told you it . . . glows," she said.

"You didn't say it lit up like a lightsaber—a red lightsaber by the way—not a good sign if you ask me."

"Take a look." Evey took the necklace off and held it out for Archer.

"No thanks," he said. "I'm definitely convinced that thing is haunted now."

Evey rolled her eyes and put the necklace back on.

"Curses aside," Archer said, "do you think this supernatural stuff about Moonlight Bluff is real? When we first talked about the Coyote Pirate protecting a secret place, I figured it was just some ancient nature preserve. But between you being in a one hundred and seventy-year-old journal, your lightsaber crystal, and . . ."

Evey noticed something out of the corner of her eye. The light from the full moon gleamed across the lake, helping her spot a red kayak in the distance. The kayaker waved. Evey rubbed her eyes to focus, but the kayaker disappeared.

"Evey, did you hear me?" Archer asked.

"Tarry," she said. "I taught I . . . saw . . . something."

"It wasn't an East Sider, was it?"

Evey laughed. "No, definitely not."

"So, what do you think? Is Moonlight Bluff really supernatural?" Archer asked again.

Evey looked at her crystal and smiled. "There's . . . something . . . magical."

"I know how to find out," Archer said. He pointed to the north end of the lake. "The journal said the creek at the north end of Coyote Bay leads the way. I bet we can find it."

Evey noticed dark storm clouds in the distance. "We've had enough . . . adventure for . . . tonight." She looked across the lake toward Grandpa's house. "Besides, we've got some crew . . . members to . . . celebrate with."

Archer nodded and moved to the back of the *Sunrise*. He grabbed the rudder handle. "Give me an order, Captain."

Evey raised the sails. "Take us . . . west—to Grandpa's."

CHAPTER 28

Howie jumped to his feet and trotted down the dock as soon as he heard Evey and Archer approaching in the *Sunrise*. Evey lowered the sails while Archer threw a rope around the dock post and pulled them in. They secured the boat and climbed onto the dock.

Howie jumped to greet Evey.

"Hey, Howie!" she said as she hugged him. The three walked to the grass where they found Alex snoring on a lounge chair.

"Alex," Evey quietly said.

Alex continued to snore.

"Alex!" Archer yelled.

"Huh?" Alex mumbled. He looked up at Evey and Archer with barely open eyes. "You're back," he said with a yawn. "Everything good?"

Evey smiled. "We . . . wrecked their boat on a . . . sandbar. So, I'd say . . . yea."

"I wish you could've seen it," Archer said. "Their boat fell completely on its side." Archer replicated the crash with his hands. "All six of them flew into the water. It was epic!"

"Cool," Alex mumbled. His eyes closed again.

Evey looked at the other lawn chairs next to Alex. "If we can't beat him—"

"Join him," Archer finished. The two took off their life vests and fell into the chairs. "Wow, that feels so much better," Archer said.

Evey nodded in agreement. Howie yawned as he snuggled her feet.

"Hey, did we beat curfew?" Archer asked.

"I . . . forgot about . . . that," Evey said.

"You're late," Alex said with his eyes still closed. "Our parents came down twenty minutes ago. They said you're both in big trouble."

Evey bit her lip. Archer scratched his neck.

"Ha—got you!" Alex said as he sat up from his chair and started laughing.

Evey threw a towel at him.

"You deserved it!" Alex replied. "You made me jump in the lake, twice!"

"For . . . somebody who loves . . . jumping off the . . . pier—"

"That's totally different!"

"Alright," Archer said, "everybody's even now."

Alex leaned back into his chair. "I'm just messing with you. Me and Howie were happy to rest. We watched you for a while, but honestly it looked kind of boring—like a slow cruise across the lake."

"Boring?" Archer said. "The waves were huge! And we smashed their boat into a sandbar! Waves—smashed—sandbar! It was like a movie!"

Alex shrugged.

Archer shook his head in disbelief.

234

"How'd it go?" boomed a voice from up the yard. Evey, Archer, Alex, and Howie all turned around to see Grandpa walking toward them with a flashlight. "Your parents sent me to make sure everybody came back okay. Did you . . ."

Grandpa paused once he saw the messy foursome. Streaks of mud and neon paint covered Evey and Archer. Alex sat wrapped in towels, and green weeds clung to Howie's white fur.

"Hi Grandpa," Evey said. "Mission . . . accomplished. Tanks for your . . . help."

"Okay—great," Grandpa said.

Evey could not tell for sure in the dark, but she thought she saw him raise an eyebrow.

"I don't think I need to know the details," Grandpa said as he headed back to the house.

Evey turned to Archer and Alex. "Speaking of tanks," she said, "I . . . I . . ."

"Spit it out, Evey," Alex said.

Evey rolled her eyes. *I really need to work on saying 'thanks,'* she thought. She rubbed her jaw. "Thank you," she slowly said. "I couldn't . . . have done it . . . without both of you."

"I'm glad to have helped," Alex said. "Honestly, tonight was way more exciting than any other Fourth of July. And you're kind of an action hero, now."

"Dare I say," Archer said, "you're the new Coyote Pirate!"

Evey smiled, then looked at her crystal. "Coyote Bay is gone," she said. "I think we . . . should be the . . . Turtle Pirates!"

"Turtle Pirates?" Alex asked.

Evey nodded. "Howie too," she said.

"Do I get a cool hat?"

"Sweet idea!" Archer said. "Like the ones in the museum. I want one."

"I don't think they make those with a Bears logo," Alex said.

"I want my own racquet," Evey said.

"That can be arranged," Archer said. "Racquets for all the Turtle Pirates! We'll be the most fearsome crew on the lake!"

The three laughed, then settled back into their chairs.

"So, Turtle Pirates, what did the big secret turn out to be?" Alex asked with a yawn.

"I almost forgot!" Evey said. "It's the Coyote Pirate's . . . journal! Do you want to tee it—I mean . . . see it?" She reached for the backpack. "It . . . tells about this place—light . . . Moonlight Bluff. He said it's spirit . . . super . . . natural. And den dare's diss photo—I mean—"

Alex began to snore. Evey looked over and saw his eyes closed. Archer's too. Even Howie was snoring by her feet.

Evey sighed, then rubbed her own heavy eyelids. *Like Archer said,* she thought, *the journal has been hidden for a hundred and seventy years. I guess it can wait.*

Evey leaned back in her chair and closed her eyes. She listened to the waves splashing against the shore. She heard crickets chirping in the yard. Her thoughts went blank and she began drifting to sleep, but a distant noise from the lake stirred her awake.

Was that howling? Evey wondered.

CHAPTER 29

Evey slept in most of the next morning. When she woke up, she talked with her parents about their fight at the park, then barely had time to peek at the Coyote Pirate's journal. Per tradition, the day after the Fourth of July, her family went mini-golfing for the last event in the Championship. In honor of Evey, Archer, and Alex finding the journal, the family chose Pirate Park for the decisive event.

The game helped distract Evey from her anxious questions about the connection between her and the Coyote Pirate. She felt so tense during the round that she told Archer and Alex to stop asking her about the journal.

Heading to the eighteenth and final hole, Evey's mom had already secured victory with three holes-in-one. Grandpa, playing better than usual after all of his practice, seemed safe in second place. However, the battle for third between Evey and her uncle would decide the Championship. Evey's pride was on the line too, as she was the only family member without a point.

Evey studied the eighteenth hole. Ponds on each side of the green left only a narrow strip of land to hit the ball through. A pirate ship swung from pond to pond, blocking the path at times.

Isn't this the hole where Grandpa fell in the pond? Evey wondered. *Never mind—focus! I'm only one shot ahead for third place.*

Archer went first. He nailed a wild shot that splashed into the left-side pond. "Penalty shot for me," he said as he used his putter to retrieve the ball. After pulling it out, he took a seat next to Evey on a bench. "I don't get it," he said. "If only your uncle or grandpa can win this silly hat championship thing at this point, why does your score matter so much?"

"Can't . . . explain," Evey said as she kept her eyes fixed on the course. "I . . . I need . . . focus."

"Oh, sorry," Archer said. He asked Alex the same question.

"It's complicated," Alex said. "For every event in the Championship, the winner gets five points, second place gets three points, and third place gets one point. Right now, my dad is in the lead with thirteen. Grandpa has eleven. In mini-golf, Evey's mom is way ahead, so she should win and get the five points. Assuming Grandpa doesn't hit his ball into the parking lot, he should get second, which would give him three points."

"I think I'm following so far," Archer said.

"With three more points," Alex continued, "Grandpa will have fourteen, putting him one ahead of my dad. But if my dad beats or ties Evey for third place in mini-golf, then he wins one point and will also have fourteen."

"Then, they'd be tied," Archer said. "Do they cut the turtle hat in half?"

Alex rolled his eyes. "If they tie, it goes to the tiebreaker," he said.

Archer scratched his neck. "Tiebreaker—do they duel with their putters?"

"No, the tiebreaker is based on who won the most events. My dad won two—board game night and ping-pong. Grandpa only won fishing."

"So, basically, if your dad ties or beats Evey, he wins the Championship. But if Evey keeps her one-shot lead, then your grandpa wins, right?"

Alex shook his head yes.

"Evey wasn't kidding," Archer said. "Your family's really into this." He turned to Evey. "Good luck, Evey!" he said with a big wave.

Evey briefly raised her eyebrow, then went back to studying the course while Grandpa lined up his first shot.

"Watch out for the ponds," Evey's uncle said. He and Evey's dad both laughed.

Grandpa ignored them while taking a few practice swings. He stepped up to the tee and hit his green ball straight and firm. It rolled past the pirate ship and landed close to the hole.

"Ha! No choking this time," Grandpa said as he winked at Evey.

Evey stood up for her turn. She dropped her red ball and took a practice swing.

"Just like we practiced!" Grandpa said nervously.

Evey nodded. She watched the pirate ship to time her shot. As soon as it swung by the narrow strip, she hit the ball. It jumped forward and rolled straight but slow. As it neared the strip between the ponds, the pirate ship started swinging downward. Her ball rolled by just before the ship could stop it, and settled about six feet from the hole.

Grandpa pumped his fist. "Nice!" he said.

"We're not done yet," Evey's uncle said as he lined up for his turn. He timed his shot perfectly and avoided the pirate ship. His ball rolled past Evey's and stopped less than a foot from the hole. "Yes!" he shouted while holding his putter in the air.

"This is intense," Archer whispered to Alex.

Evey's uncle was the first to take a second shot. He gently tapped his ball in, meaning Evey had to make her next shot to help Grandpa win the Championship. Evey's family and Archer finished their turns next to build the excitement.

"It's all up to you, Evey!" her uncle said.

"Don't bother her," Grandpa shot back.

"What? I'm just saying that if she happens to miss, there might be a reward of some . . ."

Evey tried to block out the banter and focus, but her legs felt shaky. She tried to tighten her grip on the putter, but it wiggled between her sweaty hands. She took a deep breath and stepped up to her ball. She visualized the path she wanted it to follow, then took a few practice swings.

Grandpa stood nervously, shaking his leg. "Nice and easy," he said. "Don't hit it too—"

"Shush!" Evey's mom said. "Quiet on the course."

Evey bit her lip and grabbed her crystal. *Feel free to help me on this one, Grandma,* she thought. She stepped back up to her ball. She brought her club back and swung it forward. She hit the ball straight and gently. It moved toward the hole at a painfully slow pace. The entire family held their breath as they watched the red ball crawl forward. Grandpa and Evey's uncle both grimaced. Evey watched the ball roll close to the hole. A few inches away, it nearly stopped, but suddenly fell in.

"Yes! Yes! Yes!" Grandpa shouted.

Evey's uncle shook his head in disbelief. Her parents and Archer gave her a round of high-fives.

Grandpa smothered Evey with a hug. "You're the best, Evey! I owe you everything!" he said.

Evey smiled so wide she could not speak. Once Grandpa let her go, she rubbed her jaw. "I'll . . . settle for ice cream," she mumbled.

"You got it," Grandpa said. "Chester's for everybody. I'm buying!"

Evey and her family dropped their putters off and started the short walk to Chester's.

"I'm going all in tonight," Alex said during the walk. "Two scoops of Blue Moon."

"What is Blue Moon, anyway?" Archer asked.

"You've never had it?" Alex said.

"I don't think I've ever even seen it."

"It's amazing. It tastes like a bowl of Fruity O's. You have to try it!"

Archer looked at Evey. She stuck her tongue out in disgust.

"Don't listen to her," Alex said. "She only eats vanilla."

"Evey, wait up a second," her dad said from behind her. She stopped while Alex and Archer ran ahead to Chester's. Her parents each grabbed one of her hands.

"Yea, Dad?" Evey said.

"We just wanted to, uh . . . you know . . ." her dad mumbled.

"Say thank you," her mom said. "Thank you for talking to us about yesterday. We know that was hard, but I think we all needed it. And we won't forget what you said about feeling criticized too much. We know we can be tough on you."

Evey tried to open her mouth, but her jaw felt locked. She started rubbing it, but stopped and smiled at her parents instead. *I'll remember that you said you're proud of me— with or without pirate journals,* she thought.

"Now that we got that out of the way," her dad said, "I have to say again that what you did this summer is pretty awesome."

"Really?" Evey asked.

"Of course!" her dad said. "To find the Coyote Pirate's journal from Grandma's notes—professional historians and archeologists try their whole lives to discover artifacts like that."

"Your dad's right," Evey's mom said. She stopped walking and put her hands on Evey's shoulders so they could see eye-to-eye. "But most importantly," her mom said, "we're glad you had fun doing it."

Evey felt her eyes fill with tears. She tried not to bite her lip.

Her dad cut in. "We're all excited about the journal, but look at the other cool stuff you did. You fixed up a boat and learned to sail. You researched a ton of interesting local history. You obviously improved your mini-golf skills. And you found Turtle Lake's elusive turtles, which you still need to show me, by the way. And all this time with Grandpa—I haven't seen him this happy in years."

"It has . . . been . . . fun," Evey said as she wiped a tear from her cheek.

"That's what we like to hear from you more than anything else," her mom said.

"Come here, my feisty girl!" her dad said as he and her mom opened their arms.

Evey leaned into her parents and the three hugged.

"So, what are you going to do with the journal?" Evey's mom asked once they started walking again.

"I'd love to keep it," Evey said, "but I . . . think it belongs in a . . . museum."

"Belongs in a museum!" her dad repeated. "Now you sound like Indiana Jones."

At least I've heard of that one, Evey thought. "Nineties?" she asked.

Evey's parents laughed. "No," her mom said, "that one would be the eighties. But you probably should watch those movies now that you're such an adventurer."

"Anyway," Evey said, "after I read it, I . . . will give it to the Door County . . . Historical Museum."

"Good for you," Evey's mom said.

"Come on, Evey!" Archer yelled from up ahead. "Blue Moon awaits!" Evey and her dad both stuck out their tongues at the same time.

"Go ahead," her mom said through a laugh.

Evey caught up to Archer and Alex and entered the ice cream parlor to check out the different flavors. With the holiday crowd mostly gone, the restaurant was only half full. Once their parents and Grandpa arrived, they found a patio table and ordered their desserts. Evey sat in between her dad and Archer.

Evey's dad handed the Championship turtle hat to her uncle. "Would you like to do the honors?" he asked.

Evey's uncle sighed, took the hat, and walked over to Grandpa. "Congratulations," he said as he handed the hat over with the look of a fighter giving up his belt.

Evey smiled as she and her family clapped for Grandpa.

"That's the hat you were talking about?" Archer asked.

Evey nodded. The old hat was frayed and ripped in a few spots, but still resembled a cartoonish turtle. A brown shell covered the top. A green head with two big eyes hung out the front, and four small, green legs and a tail hung out the sides and back.

"It's unique," Archer said.

Two waiters soon returned with trays full of ice cream. Archer and Alex both opted for double scoops of Blue Moon. Feeling extra celebratory, Evey chose strawberry instead of vanilla.

"Strawberry," Grandpa said, looking at the pinkish ice cream in her bowl. "Must be a special occasion."

Evey rolled her eyes.

"Speaking of that," Grandpa said, "before we dig in, I want to say something." Everybody looked at Grandpa. "I want to make a toast," he continued, "to Evey, Alex, and our new friend, Archer, for . . ." He paused as his voice cracked slightly, ". . . for reminding us all why Grandma loved it up here so much. I hope finding the Coyote Pirate's journal is the first of many adventures you three have."

Evey squeezed her fingers as everybody at the table clapped again. Looking around, she saw a lot of watery eyes.

"And one more thing," Grandpa said. "While I am very proud to have dominated in the Championship," Grandpa winked at Evey's uncle, "I believe some additional points should be awarded. I've decided, that for all of her work helping me practice mini-golf and ping-pong, not to mention fixing up Grandma's boat and finding the journal, Evey wins fourteen points."

Evey raised both of her eyebrows while doing the math in her head.

"Which means," Grandpa said as he stood up and walked over to Evey. He took the turtle hat off and placed it on her head. "Evey wins the Championship this year!"

The family cheered and clapped. Evey gave Grandpa a hug, then high-fived Archer.

"Let's eat!" Grandpa said.

Evey, her family, and Archer dug into their ice cream. *This hat is actually annoying*, Evey thought as its legs and tail flopped around her head. She chewed slowly to keep the hat still. *I need a quiet place to process the last few days*, she thought. *And read the journal—that's going to take forever! That's assuming I even want to look at that thing again. I should probably be more worried that the Coyote Pirate and I are sharing visions—or memories.*

Evey looked at her family. Her parents, aunt, and uncle talked about their morning plans before returning home the next day. Archer and Alex debated Blue Moon.

"I think it tastes more like cotton candy," Archer said. "It's good, but I wouldn't put it above Rocky Road."

"Rocky Road?" Alex replied. "I thought you had good taste."

Evey turned back to her ice cream and took a big bite. *No reason to rush anything*, she thought as she savored the creamy strawberry.

Archer nudged Evey's elbow. "Okay, Evey," he said as he and Alex leaned close to her, "the Championship is all settled, so let's see the journal. We need to start planning our trip to Moonlight Bluff."

"About that," Evey said, "I . . . uh . . . it's just . . ."

"Yes?" Alex asked impatiently.

"Over here," Evey said as she moved to the end of the table away from the adults. Alex and Archer followed. Evey pulled the journal from her backpack and carefully set it on the table. Alex took it and started flipping through the pages. "I only . . . had a little time to look," Evey said. "I kept coming back to . . . that last entry—about the loggers. I noticed something . . . weird. The date was . . . 1851."

"What's weird about that?" Archer asked.

"The letter the Coyote Pirate . . . wrote to . . . Evelyn—or me—it's dated . . . 1858."

"That is weird," Archer said. "What was he doing for those seven years? Maybe it took him that long to learn to write with his new hook hand."

Evey laughed. "And there's more," she said. "Remember how I said . . . that line in the journal . . . sounded . . . familiar? The one about . . . trying to . . . stop them."

"Yea," Archer said.

"I remembered why." Evey took a deep breath and rubbed her jaw. "Both times I talked to . . . the Coyote Pirate, the . . . vision ended with noises in the distance—like guns and . . . shouting. Both times . . . he said . . . that line about . . . stopping them." Evey took another deep breath. "I think those . . . visions were the Coyote Pirate's . . . memory of . . . the night he . . . confronted the loggers. And I think . . . there has to be a . . . reason for that."

"In your first vision, Evey," Archer said, "didn't the Coyote Pirate say he couldn't explain the secret, but that you had to experience it?"

Evey nodded.

"I'm betting that means the answers are at Moonlight Bluff," Archer said.

Alex rolled his eyes. "Archer, you do realize Moonlight Bluff is probably just a nice place to have a picnic? I'm sure there's a logical explanation behind the spooky stuff."

"What!" Archer yelled. Most of the people in the room turned to look at him. "Sorry, we're just debating ice cream flavors," he loudly said. "This Blue Moon is really something!" He turned back to Alex. "Have you listened to your cousin? Her crystal and visions, the picture of her—"

"It looks like a cartoon," Alex cut in. "It could be anybody."

Archer shook his head as he grabbed the journal and turned the pages. "Anybody!" he grumbled. "Look at this picture you close-minded, green-blooded . . ."

Evey tuned their bickering out. *I must try to stop them,* she thought, reciting the line from the journal. *The Coyote Pirate kept saying that was an important night. Something must have happened when he confronted the loggers— something that explains what he did between 1851 and 1858. Maybe the—*

A movement in the corner of Evey's eye broke her concentration. She looked outside. Across the street, a shadow-covered figure stood near the water, staring directly at her. The space around the figure looked unnaturally dark, as if it sucked all the sunlight from the sky.

Evey felt a cold chill across her neck as the figure slowly pointed a sword at her. A light flickered below her. She looked down and saw a faint red glow from her crystal. Staring at it, the sounds of the restaurant faded away. An unknown voice filled her head.

Stop him! it yelled.

"Evey?" Archer said. "You okay?"

Evey snapped out of her daze and turned back to the water. The figure had disappeared. "I . . . I . . ." she mumbled as she rubbed her eyes. "I taught I . . . saw . . . something."

"More visions of the Coyote Pirate?" Archer asked.

"No, not him," Evey said. *Stop him,* she repeated to herself. *The man with the sword—who is he?* She grabbed her crystal, which had returned to its normal, dull color, then looked at Archer and Alex. "Remember how . . . the Coyote Pirate . . . worried about bad people . . . finding . . . Moonlight Bluff?"

"Yea," Archer replied.

Evey bit her lip. "Should we?"

"What makes you think that?" Alex asked.

"Just a . . . feeling."

Archer scratched his neck. "Is it really just a feeling, or did you see something scary?"

Evey nodded. "Some . . . one," she said.

"Nonsense," Alex said. "After the craziness of last night, it's probably just your nerves. I wouldn't worry about it."

Evey looked at Alex. She raised her eyebrow.

Please Write a Review

THE END! Thank you for reading *The Turtle Pirates: Beneath the Sunrise*! Now that you finished, I need a favor! Please provide a review on Amazon as it is the best way to support independent authors like me. Plus, I love reading your feedback! If you enjoyed the book, please also share it with your friends, family, and social media channels. Your support is key in helping me write more fun stories.

If you have questions or comments on Evey, Archer, or anything *Turtle Pirates* related, you can reach out to me through my website (benswiercz.com) and Twitter (@benswiercz). And be sure to watch out for updates on future books, including . . .

The Turtle Pirates 2
Blacksmith Mansion

About the Author

Ben Swiercz is the not quite bestselling author of *The Turtle Pirates* series. Ben is also a house dad, cyclist, Lego enthusiast, mediocre cook, tower speaker snob, manual transmission snob, and lover of maps. He strongly supports team *Star Trek*. He is still recovering from the death of his turtle (cut him some slack, he had the little guy for 27 years). Ben does not like writing in the third person, which he is doing now, so he is going to stop.

Does pretending somebody else wrote your "About" page make you seem more important? I am not sure. Anyway, I (Ben) have a master's degree in history from Illinois State University. I worked in medical billing for a long time (do yourself a favor and do not ask what it is), but I decided that writing fun middle grade fiction and spending more time with my family makes me happier.

Made in the USA
Columbia, SC
21 February 2021